DEAD STRAIGHT LINE

ALSO BY MALCOLM DUFFY

Me Mam. Me Dad. Me.
Sofa Surfer
Read Between the Lies
Seven Million Sunflowers

Malcolm Duffy

DEAD STRAIGHT LINE

ZEPHYR

An imprint of Bloomsbury Children's Books

BLOOMSBURY CHILDREN'S BOOKS
Bloomsbury Publishing Plc
50 Bedford Square, London WC1B 3DP, UK
Bloomsbury Publishing Ireland Limited
29 Earlsfort Terrace, Dublin 2, D02 AY28, Ireland

First published in Great Britain in 2026 by Zephyr, an imprint of
Bloomsbury Children's Books

Text copyright © Malcolm Duffy, 2026

Malcolm Duffy has asserted his right under the Copyright, Designs and
Patents Act, 1988, to be identified as Author of this work

Extract on p.208 taken from *All Quiet on the Western Front* by Erich Maria
Remarque published by Jonathan Cape. Copyright © The estate of the late
Paulette Remarque, 1929. Translation copyright © Jonathan Cape, 1994.
Reprinted by permission of The Random House Group Limited.

This is a work of fiction. Names and characters are the product of the
author's imagination and any resemblance to actual persons, living or dead,
is entirely coincidental

All rights reserved. No part of this publication may be: i) reproduced or
transmitted in any form, electronic or mechanical, including photocopying,
recording or by means of any information storage or retrieval system without
prior permission in writing from the publishers; or ii) used or reproduced in
any way for the training, development or operation of artificial intelligence
(AI) technologies, including generative AI technologies. The rights holders
expressly reserve this publication from the text and data mining exception as
per Article 4(3) of the Digital Single Market Directive (EU) 2019/790

A catalogue record for this book is available from the British Library

ISBN (PB): 9781035919277
ISBN (ePub): 9781035919253

2 4 6 8 10 9 7 5 3 1

Cover design: Jon Gray
Typeset by Ed Pickford

Printed and bound in Great Britain by Clays Ltd, Elcograf S.p.A.

To find out more about our authors and books visit www.bloomsbury.com
and sign up for our newsletters

For product safety related questions contact productsafety@bloomsbury.com

To Tabi

'Love all, trust a few, do wrong to none.'

William Shakespeare

ONE

I DON'T HAVE trouble finding trouble.

It finds me.

I used to go looking for it.

Not any more.

I've got more trouble now than I know what to do with.

It all started with the gang.

I'm the leader, the one they follow, as if I'm a tour guide. We're not a drug gang; we don't defend our postcode. *Stay away from our numbers and letters!* We're a bunch of six guys who hang about and mess around. None of us will ever be prefects. Defects, more like it.

How come I'm the leader?

Four reasons.

One: humour.

Being funny gets you things.

Attention. Detention.

Two: I'm taller than they are.

Whether they want to or not, they have to look up to me.

Three: reckon I'm smarter than them.

My teachers reckon otherwise. They think I'm CEO of Stupid. Could be good at school if I could be bothered. I leave the bothering to others.

Want a job that brings maximum money for minimum effort, like a goalkeeper for a team that's so good, I never have to save a shot. When the ref blows for full time, I'll collect my fifty grand for keeping the goal so empty. That would be cool.

Four: I've got ideas. Tons of them.

When we're standing outside Lickin' Chicken wondering what to do next, it's me who finds a brainwave to surf in on. Usually involves something risky.

Always pushing things.

Doors.

People.

Situations.

Any road, what about the rest of the gang?

Here goes.

Barny.

Real name, Jayden Barns.

Average brain. Above average legs. Can go faster than most missiles. Never needs a bus app. He catches them no matter how far up the road they've gone. I've known Barny since, like, forever.

Mad.

Real name, Richard Maddison.

Reckon he's got Attention Seeking Disorder. Whatever gene stops you doing crazy stuff is missing from his body.

Example: we were once on a super-high roof, wondering if it was possible for a human body to leap, without the aid of rockets, to the car park opposite. Mad doesn't do wonder. He just does. Took a running jump and soared across. Must have been twenty metres to the ground. Didn't even ask us to film it. How insane is that?

Dean.

Real name, Dean Clarke.

He's the oldest of us, but not the brightest bulb in the ceiling. His parents send him to tutors to help his brain catch up. But it's lagging so far behind, they'd be better off spending their money on takeaways.

Sharky.

Real name, Finn Edwards.

Sharky's girl mad. Problem is, it's one-way traffic. None of them are bothered about him, no matter how much he combs his hair.

Then there's Yell.

Real name, Eliot Hollings.

He's the quiet one. Yell is a recent addition. Shouldn't officially be in our gang as he's in Year Ten, but he got in because I'm seeing his sister, Lauren. She asked if he could join, as he's always hanging around the house. Now he hangs around with us. Told Yell he could join on one condition. Nothing we do ever gets back to Lauren.

We don't have many rules. We're not the government. But we do have one. You gotta take part. Unfortunately, Yell doesn't seem to like this rule. Last time we jumped off Clinker's Bridge, Yell stayed dry, holding our phones. When we moved *For Sale* signs into gardens of houses that weren't for sale, Yell stood watching. A gang is not a spectator sport. He's starting to aggravate me. Being Lauren's brother does not excuse him. Time to get him off the sub's bench.

'What you doing Friday, Yell?'

He shrugs.

'Good, 'cos you and me are going on a little expedition.'

'Do I have any choice?'

Shake my head.

'You have to do it, Yell. It's the law round these parts.'

'What is it?'

'Meet me outside Soapy Suds, 7 p.m., and you'll find out.'

'What about the others?' asks Yell, looking at the rest of the gang. He bites his lower lip as if it's a chipolata.

'They've done it. Now it's your turn.'

'What we going to do?' he asks, his voice going higher with every syllable.

'DSL?'

'What's that?'

'What do you think?'

Imagine the neurons in his head breaking the speed limit as they fly about searching for the answer.

'Doing Something Lazy?'

Dean sniggers into his hand.

'Try again. And no laughing when he gets it wrong.'

Yell's nose scrunches up like a slug that's been poked with a stick.

'Demon Sticky Lasagne.'

'Not even close. Put him out of his misery, Sharky.'

'It stands for Dead Straight Line.'

TWO

YELL IS ILLUMINATED by the fluorescent lighting from the laundrette. Thought he might have pulled a sicky. But no, there he is, hopping from foot to foot, like he doesn't know which one to stand on.

I fist bump him.

'Y'all right, Yell?'

'Yeah, I'm ready.'

But he's not giving off ready vibes. Looks like he'd rather have stayed in watching Netflix in his jimmy jams.

'I was nervous the first time. But that's what tonight's all about, – giving your nerves a good work out.'

A squeaky laugh breaks from his lips.

'What's Dead Straight Line, Rory?'

Told the others not to tell him. Don't want to scare him off before it's even started.

'Very good question, Yell. Come on.' We start walking down the high street. 'It's a game I invented a few months back. It's got everything you could want – fun, excitement, exercise, only just the wrong side of legal and doesn't cost a thing, apart from a few holes in your jeans.'

'You still haven't told me what it is yet.'

'Soon, Yell, soon.'

Dead Straight Line is just one of the things we do to keep ourselves amused.

We go to parties we're not invited to. Mean, what's the point of going somewhere you know everyone? Better being the face people take notice of. Sometimes we get rumbled and thrown out. But there's always another to crash. Social is full of them. Sharky's job is tracking them down.

We do things we shouldn't. Mad's brother took a car once. We went along for the ride. Won't be doing that again. Idiot forgot to check the fuel gauge. Came to a stop on a country road, miles from town. Cost us fifty quid to get home in an Uber.

We go to movies and play Inappropriate. Wait for a really sad scene and burst out laughing. Drives people crazy.

We play Hole in One. Go to the local golf course and find a par-three hole where the golfers can't see the flag. When they hit their shots, one of us – usually Barny – rushes out from nearby bushes, puts a ball in the hole and runs back. Hard part is keeping our laughs inside as the golfer goes crazy thinking they've hit a hole-in-one.

But best of the lot is Dead Straight Line. Dean nearly bottled it the first time; said he didn't have the right gear. He didn't quit, though. Pretended to enjoy it but could tell he was loading his nappy the whole way. Still, credit to him for doing it. Mad loved it so much, he wanted to do it again, the second we finished. Reckon he does it on his own when we're not around.

'Does it last long?' asks Yell, in a voice that belongs to a Year Seven.

'Depends,' I say. 'Could be a long time, could be short. All down to what happens.'

'Is it dangerous?'

Swallow some night air. 'On a danger scale of one to ten, where one is reading a book, and ten is walking into a cage of lions wearing mince, this is… four.'

A thought hits me.

'You haven't told Lauren, have you?'

'No, said I was hanging out with you.'

'Good. Keep it that way.'

Lauren wouldn't approve. Never seen her do anything remotely bad. She even picks up litter.

'It's gonna be ace,' I say, giving Yell a playful punch.

He rubs his arm, as if I've shanked him with a blade. Never seen anyone look so terrified. Tempted to let him off, but the temptation doesn't last. Need to know what he's made of, apart from putty.

We turn off the high street into a road with houses stretching off as far as you can see.

We stop.

Take my phone out and check Google Maps.

'This'll do.'

Yell looks around, confused. 'We're gonna play the game here... in the street?'

'Yeah, this is where it starts.'

Haven't seen so much confusion on a face since Mr Hastings tried to explain heat and thermodynamics.

Time to put him out of his misery.

'Okay, Yell, here's the score. We're going to go from here, Hamilton Road, to your house in Melbourne Street. But no following footpaths, no buses, no Ubers, no detours. We go in a straight line. A dead one. Hence the name.'

For once Yell's lips stay unchewed as his mouth flops open. 'We go through people's front gardens, back gardens, over their fences?'

'Correct.'

'Isn't that trespassing?'

'Probably.'

'What if someone sees us.'

'We say we're looking for a football.'

'We haven't got a football.'

'That's why we're looking for it.'
Yell looks baffled.
'It's mad, Rory.'
'Exactly,' I say, grinning.
'How many times have you done it?'
'About twenty.'

It's closer to ten, but he doesn't need to know that. Want him to think I'm an expert at this.

'Has anything ever gone wrong?'

'No,' I lie. 'Been barked at by a couple of dogs, had a few people shout out of their windows, but most are too busy gawping at the TV. By the time they see anything on their doorbell cameras, we're on to the next garden.'

'They might see our faces.'

'Not with these they won't.'

Pull a balaclava from my pocket and hand it to Yell.

'They'll think we're burglars.'

'Yell, burglars go *into* houses, we go *around* them. And when we finish, we take the masks off and go home as if nothing happened. Do I make myself clear?'

'What's the point?'

'The point is, Yell, it's a challenge. If Mount Everest had an escalator to the top, there'd be no point in going. If the English Channel had a footbridge no one would bother swimming it. People do it 'cos it tests them.'

'Thought you said this was easy.'

'No, I said it wasn't dangerous.'

Yell seems to have shrunk. By the end of the night might have to carry him home in my pocket.

'Are you sure it's gonna be okay?'

Yell has turned into a human questionnaire.

"Course it's gonna be okay,' I shout. 'I don't do things that are impossible. Now come on, let's do it.' Find a streetlamp and show him Google Maps on my phone. 'See this house here. There's an alleyway leading to the back lane. We go down there, hop the fence into the garden of the house behind. We pick up the next alleyway and exit into Dunbar Road. Then we cross into this front garden and carry on.'

'Have you done this route before?'

'Yeah.'

A big lie wrapped in a bow. I've done Dead Straight Line a few streets from here, but not this one. That's half the challenge. Different starting points. Different routes. Different obstacles. The fun is not knowing what you're up against, trying to figure out how to stay on line.

'Okay,' I say. 'Route sorted. Now switch your phone off.'

'Why?'

'Don't want your mum saying, "Eliot, what were you doing in the middle of a back garden in Dunbar Road?" Best to switch it off for a few minutes.'

Yell takes out his phone and turns it off.

'Ready?'

Yell looks light years from ready, but he's going to do this whether he likes it or not.

'Don't want you lagging behind. Need you to stick to me like cheese to a burger.'

'Okay,' he mumbles.

Check the street to see no one's around.

'Masks on.'

We pull on our masks. Take a final look at my phone, switch it off, and we run down a garden path into an ink-black alleyway.

THREE

YELL IS BREATHING so hard you'd think he'd pressed the wrong speed on a treadmill.

'Quiet,' I whisper.

His gasping goes down a level.

Wait a second to let our eyes get used to the black. The darkness slowly peels back a layer, revealing shapes and objects and obstacles. The first is a garden fence, about two metres high.

'Let's go.'

We move down the alleyway along a gravel path.

Crunch, crunch, crunch.

Should have fitted Yell's shoes with silencers. He'd make the world's worst burglar. Can't wait until we find some lawn.

We reach the fence. Luckily, there's no barbed wire, spikes or broken glass on top. Decide to help him over. Last thing I want is me stuck on one side, and Yell stranded on the other, crying for help.

'Look,' says Yell, pointing at a sign on the fence.
Guard dogs.

'Yeah, people stick those on their fences to scare intruders away. Probably haven't even got a hamster.'

'But what if they've got an actual dog – a giant one?'

'We climb back over the fence in world record time.'

Dogs are the biggest problem with Dead Straight Line. Seems everyone's got one. While most are inside at this time of night, curled up on the sofa, farting away, some are awake four-legged listening devices, checking for strange noises and strange people. The barking's not the problem. We'll be long gone before anyone comes out to investigate. It's the dogs outside you have to worry about. Once, Mad, Dean and I landed in a garden with a human-hating Doberman. That dog was faster than all our legs put together. Me and Mad scaled the fence as if it had stopped being vertical. Dean wasn't quick enough. Got bitten on the backside. Not that he cared. Showed it off at school next day to anyone brave enough to look.

Hopefully, this will be a dog-free night. Don't fancy spending half of it in A&E waiting for Yell to get a tetanus jab in his bum.

'Okay,' I say, making a cradle with my hands.

Yell puts his foot in my hands, and I heave him to the top of the fence. A second later, he disappears over. Grab the fence, haul myself up and drop down on the other side. We crouch low, trying to keep our breaths to ourselves.

'Shit.'

'What?' mumbles Yell.

Thought the houses round here had gaps between them, but this one has built an extension. The alleyway that should lead to the street out front is gone. We could climb up a drainpipe and over the roof. But that's too crazy even for someone as crazy as me.

'Do we go back?' mutters Yell.

'No, we never go back.'

Occasionally, a Dead Straight Line has to be bent. Tonight is such an occasion. We're going to have to go into the garden next door and find another route. On our side there's a hedge so thick it looks like it came from the Amazon. On the other, there's a smaller wall of bushes.

'This way.'

The hedge is as thorny as hell. That's all part of it, though. No pain, no game. We force our way through the foliage into a garden with a small, ornamental pond gurgling away.

Do not fall in the pond, Yell.

Settle my breathing and look up at the building. No lights on. And there's a gap between it and the next-door neighbours. Our luck is in. We scoot along the side of the house, through a metal gate and into the front drive. Security lights come on as we hurry across the gravel. Not that I care. If they have cameras, they won't catch much. Two figures – one big, one small – identities unknown. We run to the street and duck behind a large hedge that hides us from the house.

Pull my mask off.

Yell stares at me with two bulging eyes.

'For god's sake,' I say, yanking the mask off his head. 'It's not Halloween.'

Nothing screams criminal more than a guy lurking next to a bush wearing a balaclava.

'Are we done now?' says Yell, lack of oxygen dicing his words.

Tempted to say yes. Yell isn't the ideal travelling companion. Too noisy, too slow, too breathy. But we've only done a couple of gardens. He hasn't proved himself yet. Don't want to tell the others I failed to get him round. We're going all the way to Melbourne Street whether he likes it or not.

We're in Dunbar Road now. On the other side of the street the houses are bigger, swankier. That means more security, but it also means something else: bigger gardens, more entry and exit points. Swings and roundabouts, as Mum says.

Check Google Maps.

'We'll go this way,' I say, pointing at the house opposite.

'How many more gardens do we have to cross?' asks Yell.

'No idea. I'm not a town planner. But don't worry, the more you do, the easier it gets.'

Turn my phone off and we cross the road.

Check the house.

'Looks perfect,' I whisper. 'No lights on, no cars in the drive, big garden.'

'What if they have dogs?'

'I'll give 'em some dog food.'

Yell is seriously starting to annoy me.

Check the street. An old guy is out walking a tiny dog. More like a rat on a rope. Hope he's the owner of the house. Wait until he's out of sight before we put our masks on.

'Let's go.'

Slowly lift the latch on the metal gate. Someone has kindly oiled the hinges. Not a squeak. Close the gate and hurry down the path at the side of the house. No security lights come on. So far, so good. There's a wooden gate. Give it a push. It stands firm. Got one of those combination locks on it.

'What's the code?' asks Yell.

'How the hell would I know?'

'Look,' he says, pointing at a sign: *Premises covered by CCTV.*

'Until someone invents a camera that can see through balaclavas, we're fine.'

I wheel a recycling bin over to the gate. Yell climbs on top and hops over. I follow. Find ourselves in a sprawling back garden with a hot tub, swimming pool, garden room. Things I'll have once my goalkeeping career takes off. But we aren't here to house hunt. Need to get in and out as quickly as possible. Speed is key to success in Dead Straight Line.

I sprint across the lawn to the bottom of the garden.

Hear Yell not far behind.

Panting hard.

We're met by a wall of green.

Need a machete to get through it.

'We're trapped,' gasps Yell.

'No, we're not.'

After the last detour I'm determined to find a way out of this place. The name of the game is not Dead Wonky Line. Search the grounds. The only way to the next house over is via the roof of the garden room, but it's a lot higher than any of the fences we've tackled.

'We'll climb over here,' I whisper.

'How?'

Look around the garden for something to help us over the top. Finally spot it, in a corner by the hot tub.

'Grab the table.'

We each take an end of the wooden table and carry it across the lawn, plonking it next to the garden room.

'Now what?' goes Yell, his breaths coming hard and fast.

'We sit down and have a barbecue.' Shake my head. 'We climb on the table, get on the roof and jump into the garden behind.'

Don't need to be fluent in body language to know Yell isn't happy. I grab him by his slumped shoulders.

'We're not going back, Yell. You are doing this.'

A small nod from balaclava boy.

'Up you go.'

Yell climbs on to the table and manages to pull himself on to the flat roof. He makes his way gingerly to the back, overlooking the neighbour's garden.

'It's a long way down,' he mutters.

What's the matter with this kid? Wait until he does Clinker's Bridge. Ten metres into cold water. Now that's a jump.

I climb on to the table and haul myself on to the roof. Yell is standing by the edge, like a statue.

'Just jump.'

'It's too far.' He peers over the edge. 'Can't see what's down there.' It's a garden. What does he expect, a shark-infested lake?

'We are *not* going back, Yell.'

As things stand, we're not going forward either. Starting to get nervous. If he's right about the CCTV sign, someone may have already clocked us. They could be heading outside, or on the phone to the police.

Need to keep moving.

'You've got to go, Yell.'

'Don't want to.'

'We can't stay here all night. You've got to jump.'

But gravity has him in its grasp.

'Go for it, Yell.'

A second later, it's over.

He's vanished.

Hear a dull thud as he makes contact with whatever's down below. Probably landed in a hedge, or a pile of compost.

'Rory,' he screams.

'Shut up,' I say as loud as I dare.

'Rory,' he screams even louder.

If there's anything guaranteed to get lights switched on, dogs barking and 999 dialled, it's a stranger at the bottom of your garden screaming 'Rory'.

Make my way over to the edge and look down. Blackness. Don't like turning my phone on mid-game but need to know what's happened. Power it up, turn on the torch and point the beam into the garden. Yell is lying on a pile of rubble.

At an angle that doesn't look right.

'Rory,' he shouts again.

'Shut up. I'm coming.'

He wasn't wrong. It is a long way to the bottom. Hang off the edge of the roof and drop down. Land on a big pile of stones. Stumble when I hit the ground but manage to keep my balance.

'I'm hurt,' he shouts.

Lights come on in the house.

'Shit.'

Need to stick to the script.

We're looking for our football.

Our invisible football.

Yell's lying on his back, staring straight at the stars.

'Get up,' I shout.

'I can't.'

'What do you mean, you can't?'

Turn the torch on him. Through the slits in his balaclava I see his eyes.

Burning with fear.

'My legs. I can't move them.'

FOUR

'WHY, WHY, WHY?'

The same question punches me in the face, over and over.

And always the same answer.

'Don't know, don't know, don't know.'

Even though I do.

I don't like being told what to do.

I like the respect that comes from the guys, knowing another rule has been successfully broken.

Most of all, I love the buzz, doing the sort of stuff people chained to their sofas would never dream of doing. In a world of boring, I want breathtaking, bum clenching. I want to get into my discomfort zone.

But this time I've gone too far.

Didn't mean any harm. Apart from spooking a few dogs, some crushed plants, battered hedges, rearranged garden furniture and torn jeans, I'd done nothing wrong.

Until now.

It's been four days since I took Yell on Dead Straight Line.

Mum and Dad took my phone and laptop off me. Probably the closest you can get to hitting your child, without actually hitting them. I love my phone. Hate it too. Like a friend who's also an enemy. Know there'll be good stuff, people backing me up. But among it will be the garbage, the lies, abuse, gossip, hate, rumours. Which side will Lauren be on? She knows I'd never hurt her brother. She also knows I was responsible for him getting hurt.

Mum and Dad have grounded me, like I can't be trusted to walk out of the front door and not cause mayhem. I'm trapped in my centrally heated, fully carpeted, suburban prison. I fill in my days working on my core strength, listening to music, thinking about Yell and Lauren, and feeling sick.

What the hell's happened to Yell? No one's told me anything since the night he got taken away in the ambulance.

I'm doing a wall squat when I see the handle turn.

The door opens slowly.

Has to be Mum. Dad would have kicked it in.

'What are you doing?' she asks, standing at the door, arms folded.

'Working on my thighs.'

My personal best is three minutes twenty. I'm trying to break four.

'Can you stop that, please?'

Gladly. My legs are vibrating as though they've got their own earthquakes. Move away from the wall and sit on the bed, rubbing my thighs. Mum comes in and sits next to me. Think for a second she's going to hug me, but she keeps her arms to herself. Can tell from her face the news is not good.

'What?'

Mum looks out of the window. I steel myself for what's coming, the blow that might knock me into next week. Her voice is quiet, as if she can't bear anyone hearing what she has to say next.

'I heard from Mrs Hollings… He's never going to walk again, Rory. Eliot's going to spend the rest of his life in a wheelchair.'

I bend over, crushed by that ten-letter word.

Wheelchair.

'Can't be true.'

'It is.'

'It was only a small jump.'

'Not small enough.'

'Shit.'

Yell's never going to walk or run or skip or hop or climb. The wheelchair is going to be part of him. Forever. Feel like I did the day Grandad died. Only worse. Because there was nothing I could do about Grandad. Dementia took him. Yell's accident is down to me. I'm the one who got him to do Dead Straight Line. I'm the one who helped him on to that roof. Feel like I'm in a scene from a movie I don't want to be in. Need the script to flip back twenty pages to when it was me and the gang, messing around. When no one got hurt. But the scene's not going to change. Yell's got his part and I've got mine. The lad in a wheelchair. And the lad who put him there.

Before Mum came to my room there was hope that Yell might be okay; that he had a bad fracture or something; that after a few days in bed he'd get the feeling back in his legs and be up and running. I tried to imagine him into being all right. But the longer it went without any news, the more I realised Yell was not going to be okay. Mum's words have trampled hope into dust.

'Is there any chance he'll walk again?'

'Doesn't look like it.'

'Who told you?'

'Mrs Hollings. But wasn't so much told, as screamed at.' Mum looks outside, tears blurring her view. 'She said they'd carried out a ton of tests. His nerve fibres are all damaged.'

'Can they fix them?'

'She said other things about his lower spinal cord,' says Mum, ignoring my question. 'She was shouting and crying so much I couldn't understand her. Then she hung up on me.'

'I'm sorry, Mum.'

And this time her arms envelop me, squeezing out tears. Can't remember the last time I cried, but they come in a flood, as if they've been saving themselves for this moment. Mum joins in, and we grip each other tight, sobbing, sobbing, until we can sob no more.

I break from her and blow my nose on a tissue.

'Does Dad know?'

'Not yet. Need to call him.'

'It was just a game.'

Mum blows her nose too and puts her hands on her knees.

'Could you not have found something else to do, Rory?'

Maybe. But what? We're sixteen. Too young for pubs, too old for playgrounds. There's only so long you can hang around a shopping centre. Guess we could have found hobbies, but that would mean turning up and practising and following rules. And we weren't the turning up, practising, following rules sort of guys. Mad had played football for the school but got thrown out for arguing with the ref. Sharky had practised piano until his moaning got worse than his playing, and his parents let him stop. The rest of us preferred messing around.

'That's not all, Rory. There's more bad news.'

Can there be anything worse than losing the use of your legs aged fifteen?

But this wasn't about Yell as it turned out.

It was about me.

'His mum said something else.'

Swallow spit.

'Eliot said you pushed him off the roof.'

FIVE

HER WORDS MAKE me want to throw up. Not that I've got anything to eject. Barely eaten a thing since that night.

'Pushed?'

'That's what she said.'

'It's not what happened. Mum, he's lying.'

'Why would he do that?' she says, staring at me. Into me.

'To take the blame off him and put it on me.'

She shakes her head. Not sure if it's because of the situation I'm in, or because she doesn't believe me.

'Eliot's mum also told me what you and your mates get up to.'

How much more bad news can one day hold? Yell has become chief witness for the prosecution.

Should never have let him join the gang.

He's a good guy. Won't cause any trouble.

Thanks, Lauren.

Mum glares at me.

'Not only this Dead Straight Line nonsense, but jumping off Clinker's Bridge, gate-crashing parties, stealing *For Sale* signs. What the hell? You told me you hung around their houses, playing video games.'

'We did. Sometimes.'

'And the rest of the time?' says Mum, her face screwed up, as if I'm roadkill. 'You were causing chaos in the neighbourhood.'

I grip the edge of the bedframe. 'Okay, we did some crazy stuff. But I didn't push him off the roof.'

She wipes her eyes. 'I want to believe you.'

'Want to?'

'Yes, Rory, with all my heart, but how can I know for certain, after what I've found out? I thought I knew you.'

Mums stand by their sons. Isn't that what they do? But her loyalty's been trampled on by my lies, half-truths. Yell has told his parents everything me and the guys got up to. Why should she believe a single thing I say?

Another thought hits me hard. If Mum knows, Lauren knows.

Look after my brother.

And look how I repay her. How can I even speak to her? Almost glad I haven't got my phone.

'I did stupid stuff, Mum, but I'm not a psychopath.'

'Not saying you are. All I know is Eliot Hollings is in a wheelchair because of you.'

'No, he's in a wheelchair because he fell on to a pile of concrete.'

'Because of an insane game you made him play.'

'Didn't make him. He was up for it.'

'That's not what I've heard.'

'From who?'

'People.'

'Which people?'

'I'm not naming names.'

'Dean, Barny, Mad, Sharky?'

'I said I'm not naming names.'

Mum must have spoken to their parents. One of the guys will have cracked, told his parents how I invented Dead Straight Line; how I wanted Yell to do it, to prove himself, show he was fit to be in the gang. All roads lead to me.

'What did they say?'

'That you pressurised Eliot into doing it.'

'How exactly did I do that? Put a gun to his head, threaten him with a blade?'

'I'm only the messenger, Rory.'

Silence fills the space.

'I'm sorry,' I sigh.

'You don't sound sorry.'

'Sorry for not sounding sorry, but I'm angry, Mum. People out there are liars.'

'Guess it takes one to know one.'

She stares at me, but there's no love in her look. Not even hate. It's something else. Disgust. As if she wished I wasn't here. As if she wished I'd never been born.

'What are we going to do with you?'

'You can start by believing me. I didn't push him. I swear.'

'I pray that's true, Rory.' She blows her nose again and walks to the door. 'Can you change out of your sweatpants?'

'Why?'

'The police are coming round.'

SIX

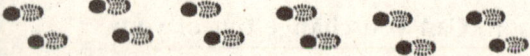

TELL THE POLICE all about Dead Straight Line.

They listen with dead straight faces.

Don't bother with the football excuse. Who'd believe two guys were looking for a football in a back garden half a mile from their house? Not even a world-class goalie kicks the ball that far. Nor did I mention the rest of the gang. Yell has already dobbed us all in and told them about what we did, while he held our phones, like the perfect innocent bystander.

'Why were you so keen for Eliot to take part in this game?' asks a young woman police officer with a notepad balanced on her knee.

'It's our favourite. Everyone had done it apart from Yell, I mean, Eliot. He wasn't getting involved, and we thought it would be good if he did.'

'We?'

'Mostly me.'

'He was happy to play the game?'

'Wouldn't say happy, but he agreed.'

'Tell us what occurred on the roof of the garden room.'

This is what they'd come for. The main event. Not to find out about two guys jumping over fences. Obviously had better things to do. They wanted to know what happened on that roof.

The push.

Versus the jump.

Mum and Dad hunch forward, fingers knotted, fear lighting their eyes, as if I'm in the dock, not perched on our lumpy sofa with a plate of ginger biscuits in front of me. Dad still wears that look of fury he had when Mum broke the news. They were no hugs, no tears, when he got home. Instead, there was an hour of yelling that left my ears ringing.

Sit up straight to deal with the police officer's question. The most important I've answered in sixteen years.

'Me and Eliot were trying to find a way out of the garden. The hedges were too high, too thick to crawl through. Thought we might find a way over via the garden-room roof, but it was impossible to climb up. No hand holds, no nothing. I saw a wooden table. We carried it over. Eliot climbed up first.'

'Was he happy to climb?'

'He had to be. It was the only way out.'

'You could have gone back.'

'We never do that.'

'Then what happened?' asks the police officer.

'Eliot got scared. Said it was too high.'

'And what did you do?'

'Climbed on the roof, to encourage him.'

'But he still wouldn't move?'

'No.'

'So how did he end up in the garden of Mr and Mrs Claymore?'

'He jumped.'

'Of his own accord?'

'Yes.'

'You didn't push him?'

'No.'

'Nudge him?'

'No.'

'Not even the slightest poke?'

'No, wasn't even in touching distance. I said we needed to get a move on, that it wasn't far down to the garden.'

'It was three metres.'

'That's what I mean.'

'Long way for a small lad.'

'Thought he'd land on something soft.'

'Did you not think to look?'

'No. I've jumped into loads of gardens. Never had

anything like this happen. Thought it would be grass or a hedge, a pile of leaves or something. Had no idea there were rocks there.'

They stare at me with their specially trained police eyes, trying to see inside my brain. Glad they didn't bring a heart rate monitor. My beats per minute would have broken it.

'And when he jumped, if he jumped, what did you do then?'

'Eliot started screaming. Knew something was wrong. Turned my phone on. Saw him lying on the rocks, all twisted. Lowered myself down. That's when people came running from the house. Someone called an ambulance.'

Don't need to say any more. Everyone knows how the story ends.

The police officer closes her pad.

'Thanks, Rory.'

'What happens now?' asks Mum, looking at the police officers as she wrings her hands.

'We'll be in touch.'

SEVEN

THE NEXT FEW days last a month.

Mum spoke to school and they agreed it's best if I stay at home. It's hell. Without any means of communication; no idea what's going on. Guesswork is the only work I can do. The second I get my phone back I'm going to spend a full day wearing my thumbs out.

Wonder what the police are doing with their investigation. If this ever goes to court, hope Mum and Dad aren't on the jury. They already treat me as though I'm guilty. The atmosphere in our house is toxic. Dad looks like he can't bear to breathe the same air as me. Mum goes silent whenever I appear and busies herself with something. Try to engage with Poppy, my younger sister, to find out what's going on, but Mum always intervenes, as though I'll lead Poppy astray and make her jump through hedges. Even our dog, Biscuit, seems to have picked up on the vibes and looks at me as if I've eaten all his food.

I'm the same Rory as before, but they treat me as if there's a different person in the house. A Rory who's dangerous, can't be trusted. Who can blame them? They reckon I pushed him. It's Yell's word against mine. A straight-A student who never puts a foot wrong, versus a guy who never puts his feet right.

Beat my brain up for answers to how pushy I was. The answer is always the same. I didn't force Yell into doing it. Simply told him to meet me outside Soapy Suds. He could have bailed any second he liked.

That's not to say I'm innocent.

It was my game.

It was my idea to get him to do it.

It was my idea to climb on the roof.

Guilt.

Felt it tons of times before. Nothing like this, though. It's a constant companion, sleeping with me, invading my dreams, waking up next to me, following me. I sometimes forget about it. For maybe a second. But that's all. One out of the 86,400 seconds that fill my day. Charities make appeals for all sorts of things, but no one ever raises money for victims of guilt. Guess, unlike those who get sick, the guilty ones deserve it. We brought it on ourselves. Our own acts have branded us.

Should never have got Yell to play the game.

The stupid game.

The bedroom door opens. Sit up straight as Mum and Dad appear, with matching red eyes and pale faces, as if they've been up all night binge-watching horror movies. Their expressions don't fill me with confidence. Feel like a guy on death row whose pardon got lost in the post. The sandwich I swallowed earlier makes an appearance at the back of my throat. Manage to hold it down. They've come to tell me about the police.

'Are they gonna charge me?'

They both shake their heads.

'It's not about the police.'

Mum does that. Starts a sentence. Then leaves it hanging. Like a noose.

'Then who is it about?'

'Mr Thomas, your headteacher.'

'What about him?'

'We've spoken to him.'

'He doesn't want you back,' says Dad, finishing what Mum started.

'He thinks I pushed Yell?'

Dad swivels his wedding ring round and round his finger. 'Yes.'

'Thought school believed in facts over fake,' I say, clenching my fists. 'Isn't that what they're always banging on about? Don't believe in hearsay or rumours, they say. Look at the evidence.'

'Verbal evidence is still evidence, Rory,' says Mum, turning into a lawyer.

The motto at my school, Copsem High, is *Veritas*, Latin for truth. Ironic, or what?

Wonder if anyone's defended me. The gang know I'd never push Yell, but guess the last thing they want right now is to turn the spotlight on themselves by supporting me.

'Can't believe you've done this,' says Dad. 'In your GCSE year.'

Makes it sound like I had it all planned. Avoid my exams by getting kicked out of school for throwing my girlfriend's brother off a roof.

Grip the edge of my bed. 'I didn't do it,' I scream.

'Unfortunately, your school thinks otherwise,' says Mum.

'I'm just glad he hasn't passed his driving test,' says Dad. 'The thought of him at the steering wheel, a car full of lads, a hundred miles per hour, straight over roundabouts. Doesn't bear thinking about.'

Guess I won't be getting driving lessons for my seventeenth birthday.

'Have you spoken to Dean's mum?'

Mum and Ellie Clarke are close. Go to Pilates every Friday; book club once a month.

'Yes, I've spoken to her. She told me she wants you nowhere near her son.'

The punches keep on coming.

'They know all about your games, Rory,' says Mum, spit glossing her lips. 'You are so juvenile.'

As in delinquent.

Sixteen going on six.

'What about the other guys?'

'No, Rory,' shouts Dad. 'Can you get it into that thick head of yours we don't want you going anywhere near them.'

'But they're my friends.'

'Friends like that you can do without. It's over.'

I'm in a gang of one.

EIGHT

THE ONLY GOOD thing to come out of Dead Straight Line is that it taught me how to move stealthily. Wearing my sound-cancelling slippers, I sneak along the hall to the top of the stairs. Don't need to watch TV to witness a family drama. There's one going on in my house every night. Hold on to the banister and listen to the latest instalment.

'Where did we go wrong, Alan?'

'Who's we? He did this all by himself.'

'He's our son. We brought him up. We have some responsibility.'

'No, we don't, Tara. Do you think the parents of serial killers blame themselves for what their kids did?'

'Some of them.'

Dad bats away her observation with a short, sharp laugh. 'I'm not getting into that nature–nurture rubbish. He's sixteen. Old enough to know better.'

'What were you like at that age?'

'Smoking cigarettes was as bad as it got.'

'Well, weren't your parents the lucky ones.'

'I'm not taking an ounce of blame for what that idiot did. He brought this on himself.'

A pause.

One without adverts.

'We should have set tighter boundaries,' says Mum. 'He was going out an awful lot, coming back all dirty. Said they'd been playing football. We should have checked to see where he was.'

'Don't forget it was you who said how good it was, him hanging out with his mates, getting fresh air, instead of stuck in his room, glued to his phone.'

'Oh, so it's my fault, is it?'

'Never said that.'

'You could have given him more attention.'

'Why me?' shouts Dad.

'You're both males.'

'With a thirty-year age gap. I offered to teach him golf and he looked at me as if I was from Mars.'

Another pause.

'Who knows what else he's done he hasn't told us about,' says Mum. 'Do you think he's involved in drugs? Sam and Lisa's lad got caught dealing dope outside the station.'

'Don't you think pushing a kid off a roof is enough?'

'We don't know he did that,' says Mum.

Dad's silence tells me he's already made his mind up.

'What are we going do if the police find video evidence?'

'Then it's game over,' sighs Dad. 'He'll not be able to talk his way out of that.'

For once I hope the house does have a camera, showing exactly what happened on the roof that night. But knowing my luck it'll be broken. Or doesn't exist.

Think they're as angry with themselves, as me. They only had two kids to keep an eye on. How could they not spot one of them had gone off the rails? Maybe it's because I'm a guy who never came home stupidly late or stupidly drunk and always had a believable story for what I was up to. Whatever the reason, they never seemed worried about me.

Now all they do is worry.

I'm their only topic of conversation, taking me everywhere with them. From the sitting room, to the kitchen, up the stairs and into the bedroom, where they carry on talking about me late into the night and probably into their dreams. Guess it's shame that's eating them up. While most of their friends have kids looking at predicted grade 9's, their son is looking at a predicted prison sentence.

Be different if I was older. But I'm not. They're my guardians. On top of that, they've got roles that demand good behaviour. Mum sits on the board of governors at Poppy's old primary school. Dad sits on the local council. They want a quiet, respectable, suburban life, where the worst that can happen is a parking ticket or a fine for going five miles over the speed limit. I've put a bundle of explosives under the floorboards and blown their lives sky high.

*

Spend the next few days worrying myself sick about what's going to happen.

Finally, I get the answer.

The door opens. Mum and Dad are back. Try to read their expressions. Can't.

'The police have been in touch,' says Dad. 'They've decided not to press charges.'

I leap from my bed and punch the air.

'Yes.'

Perhaps I should have said 'no'.

My parents stand there, glaring at me. They're not in the air-punching mood. Apart from Dad, who looks as if he wants to punch *me*.

Sit back down.

'This is no cause for celebration,' he says.

''Course not. What did they say?'

Mum joins me on the bed. 'With Eliot willingly taking part in your game and no evidence that he was pushed, the Crown Prosecution Service have said there is no case to answer.'

'It might have been different if they'd had witnesses or CCTV,' goes Dad, who almost sounds disappointed they didn't.

The owners of 16 Dunbar Road must have spent all their money on the pool, hot tub and garden equipment. They could afford the CCTV sign, but not the CCTV to go with it. The Crown versus Rory Gordon was a contest no one would ever get to see.

'Does that mean I'm not grounded any more?' I ask.

'No,' exclaims Dad.

'If I'm not guilty, I go free, right?'

Dad releases a bitter little laugh. 'You are so guilty, Rory Gordon. Thanks to you a young lad will never walk again. You are staying in this house until we say otherwise.'

NINE

IT'S DAY FOURTEEN when I'm finally freed.

'I need some bits and pieces from the supermarket,' says Mum, handing me a list.

'You not coming?'

She shakes her head. 'Got a plumber booked. Unfortunately, they never tell you when they'll arrive, as if I've got nothing better to do than hang around all day waiting for them.'

Mum is letting me out. On my own.

'Does Dad know?'

'He does. We spoke about it, last night.'

It took a family board meeting to decide whether I can go to the shops. What's my world come to? Suppose the supermarket is as good a place as any to start. Hardly likely to meet anyone. Guys like me don't hang around there. And it's two o'clock in the afternoon. Everyone will be at school.

'Will you drop me there?'

'Rory, how many times do I have to tell you, I need to stay in for the plumber. If I pop out for one second, that will be the second he turns up.'

'Will you book an Uber?'

'You are not getting an Uber to the shops. You've got legs. Use them.'

Wish she hadn't said that.

She hands me a list, some cash and her loyalty card.

'Can I have my phone?'

'No.'

End of conversation.

I go to my wardrobe, find a hoody scrumpled on the floor and sling it on. I put the list, the cash, the card in my pocket, go downstairs, grab some bags, head for the front door. Then stop. I've jumped off bridges into icy water, climbed over walls with barbed wire on top, dived through hedges full of thorns, but somehow I can't turn a handle.

The door isn't the problem, it's what lies on the other side.

People.

With eyes and mouths and phones and opinions.

It's him. The one who pushed that young lad off the roof.

Pull my hoody up and step outside. The supermarket is about a mile away as the crow flies. Not that I'll be following any crows today. To keep everyone happy I need to travel the way normal people do – on pavements. Hurry along, eyes down, occasionally looking up to make sure I don't headbutt a lamp-post.

Reach the supermarket, grab a trolley and go inside. The place is cool. I'm glad. Can dry up some of the sweat that's currently pooling in my crevices. Better still, it's quiet; only a few people here and there, peering at boxes, tins, packages, hoping for a bargain.

Grab Mum's list and start wandering about. Hardly ever shop, and everything is where I least expect it. But don't care how long it takes to track down, I'm not asking anyone for help. After more laps than an F1 driver, I get the last thing on the list – a large tin of baked beans – and head towards the self-checkout.

'Rory.'

My stomach flips like a gymnast.

Lauren.

Tempted to abandon my trolley and make a run for it. But Mum needs her shopping. And I need to find some courage.

'Why aren't you at school?' I blurt.

'Why aren't you in prison?'

Lauren pushes her trolley towards me. Looks totally different from the last time I saw her. No make-up. No nail extensions. Hair all over the place, as if she's been hedge-diving. But it's her anger that really shines through. Face flushed red from neck to forehead; lips I'd kissed, now ready to spit on me; eyes I'd gazed into, now narrow slits. She bashes her trolley into mine, like the dodgems have come to town.

'You've got a nerve showing your face,' she shouts. 'Have you any idea what you've done to my little brother?'

She bashes into me again for good measure.

'He didn't have to come with me.'

Lauren laughs. 'That's so not Eliot's story. Said you pushed him into it. That he didn't want to, but *you* made him.'

Only wanted to see if he'd got the nerves, the balls, the guts, the backbone – whatever part of the anatomy stands for bravery. That's all.

'Ask the rest of the gang what happened.'

'I have. They said you wanted him to prove himself, that you were sick of him not joining in.'

'I didn't force him.'

'Why didn't you warn him? He had no idea what you had planned. He didn't even have his trainers on. He had his school shoes. You made him wear a balaclava; took him over fences and hedges. You know he's not sporty. Then you dragged him on to the roof of a massive garden room. He hates heights.'

'Never said that.'

'Didn't you think to ask?'

No.

'I'd never do anything to hurt him.'

'Then why did you push Eliot off the roof?'

Wondered how long that would take to surface.

'Didn't.'

Lauren's knuckles turn white as she grips the handle of her trolley. 'You calling my brother a liar?'

Shake my head.

'Then why did you do it?'

Deep breath.

I'm not going to take this.

'Sorry, Lauren, but your brother is lying. Maybe he got confused after what happened.'

'Eliot damaged his spinal cord. There's nothing wrong with his head. He looked up to you, Rory. I thought you'd be a role model for him. You promised me you'd take care of him.'

'I did.'

'By paralysing him?'

Feels like the day Mum broke the news.

Only worse.

Lauren is also a victim of that night.

'It was your game,' she shouts. 'You were in charge. You were the older guy. Shouldn't you have checked where you were taking him?'

'I didn't know what was on the other side of that drop.'

'You had a phone. Why didn't you shine it down there?'

'Didn't want us to get caught.'

'You are so unbelievably selfish,' she screams. 'You risked my brother's life for your own amusement.'

Shoppers are avoiding our aisle, not wanting to get caught up in the war that's kicked off next to the pet food. For the last two weeks, I've been desperate to get out of my house. Now all I want is to go back there.

'I'm sorry, Lauren.'

She crumples over the handle of her trolley, as though she's got a bad cramp. Tears flow down her face, on to a box of cornflakes. A young shop assistant scurries over and puts a hand on her shoulder. Her badge tells me she's called Faye.

'Y'all right, love?'

Lauren shakes her head.

'Is she a friend of yours?' asks Faye, looking at me.

'Was,' I mumble.

'Would you like me to get you a chair?'

Lauren straightens up. 'No, I do not want to sit down. He' – she shouts, pointing at me – 'he has put my brother in a wheelchair. He's never gonna walk again.'

Faye turns her eyes on me. Not the friendly shop assistant any more. 'What did you do?' she says, eyebrows arching.

Didn't come here to talk about that night. I came here for toilet rolls and beans and bananas and tomatoes. I so want to get out of here.

'Can you leave us alone, please?' I mutter.

Faye nods, only too happy to go back to stacking shelves. Lauren's tears continue. I want to hold her, wrap her in my arms, but there are two trolleys between us and a gulf that's way too big to be bridged. We're never going to be close again.

She wipes her eyes. 'You didn't even bother to contact me.'

'My parents took my phone and my laptop.'

'You could have written.'

'A letter? Who writes letters?'

'Duh, you. The guy who destroyed my brother.'

She's right. I could have written. It wouldn't help Yell walk, but it might have made Lauren and her family realise how sorry I am, and that I'd do anything, *anything*, to make amends. And it would all be written down, like a peace treaty.

Not that there'd ever be any peace.

'I didn't think it was dangerous.'

'You idiot, Rory. I'll show you dangerous,' says Lauren, grabbing her phone from the back pocket of her jeans. She turns it to me, swiping through endless pictures of Yell in hospital, wires coming from him, his face crushed by what's happened below his waist. 'This is what dangerous looks like. This, and this and this,' she says, as she continues to swipe. 'He's now a paraplegic. The fall on those bricks damaged his thoracic spine between nerves T_1 and T_6. He's got no feeling below his waist. His bladder and bowel are screwed. This is all your doing.'

It doesn't seem possible. Such a small fall. Such big consequences. The garden we'd jumped into was having a renovation job. It was only when it was flooded with light that I finally saw what we'd landed on. A huge pile of bricks and masonry. That's what did for Yell.

And me.

If I could live that night again, there's so much I'd change. I'd make sure he was one hundred per cent happy to do Dead Straight Line. I'd make Yell go home and get some trainers. I'd check the drop from the garden room. I'd go first, to make sure everything was okay.

But that ship has sailed.

And sunk.

'Do you know the biggest joke of all?' says Lauren. 'I thought it would be super cool for Eliot to hang out with you. Ha, what a joke. He's ten times more mature than you'll ever be. Now he struggles to get out of bed. Why the hell didn't you tell me what you were up to?'

'Cos you might have stopped me.

And I didn't want that.

I'd been leading two lives: the one where I took Lauren out and stuck to the rules, and the other one, where the rule book got shredded.

I loved life number two.

The excitement of it.

Lauren would never understand.

Not even sure I understand.

'I'm sorry, Lauren. The game was my idea, but I didn't make Yell do it. The police have said they're not going to press charges.'

Lauren scowls at me.

'You think you're in the clear, don't you? Just you wait. You are so going to pay for this.'

TEN

FEEL I'VE ALREADY paid.

Ten times over.

My body drained by remorse.

My brain battered by guilt.

My life crushed by accusations.

But Lauren's not going to settle for that. She wants blood. And she knows people who can get it. She has a cousin in the military: Andy, the size of a Humvee. Saw him at a barbecue at hers, opening beer bottles with his teeth. He would murder me in a fight. He's not the only one. Lauren has access to an entire army. I remember being at another party at hers. Standing room only. Asked her if she'd invited the whole street. No, she told me, they're all my relatives. Lauren doesn't have a family tree, she has a family forest.

Lauren and I had so much in common. Now the only thing we share is guilt. Her for getting her brother involved, me for not taking care of him. Should never have got Yell involved. Instinct told me it was wrong. He was like a piece from the wrong jigsaw. I wanted to please Lauren, though, and if I'd refused, she'd want to know why. Me and the guys weren't watching age-relevant movies or making TikToks; we were out bending rules, until they snapped. She knew I liked a laugh but had no idea the laughs came with an added dose of danger.

The only pin-sized positive I can take from bumping into her is that it won't happen again. Our relationship is over.

I'm going to miss her.

We'd only been going out six months. Met her at a party I wasn't meant to be at. Me and Sharky sneaked in. Party wasn't great, but we stayed, hoping it might improve. Got a theory about parties. The longer you're there the more likely you are to meet people like you, who'd rather be out having fun, than stuck at home, having none.

And so it proved.

It was gone midnight when I met Lauren in the queue for the loo. She looked amazing, in a dress forever hanging in my memory wardrobe. Had the most incredible green eyes. Still has, in fact. She was a bit drunk and needed a wall to keep her vertical. Someone was throwing up in the toilet.

'Thought those sausage rolls looked dodgy,' I said.

She laughed and took a sip from her wine glass. 'Are you a friend of Sophie's?' she asked.

To lie, or not to lie, that was the question.

Got struck down by a rare case of honesty.

'No, I'm a gatecrasher.'

She giggled, thinking I was joking. Then stopped, realising I wasn't.

'You actually gatecrashed?'

Nodded.

'How'd you get past the guy with the guest list?'

Same technique as usual. Climbed over the back-garden fence.

She doesn't need to know that.

'Told him I'm here to unblock the toilet.'

Another laugh.

'I'm Lauren.'

'I'm Rory.'

'Nice to meet you, Rory.'

We shook hands.

The toilet door flew open. The guy who'd eaten the dodgy sausage roll staggered out, looking in need of a bed and a bucket. We watched as he pinged off the walls like a squash-ball and tumbled down the corridor.

'Like me to hold your glass?'

'Sure.' I took it from her. 'Wish me luck,' said Lauren as she held her nose and went inside.

I looked at her glass. A lipstick smudge on the rim. I kissed the mark her lips had made. Might be the closest I'd get to the real thing. She'd laughed about the gatecrashing, but it could have been a 'you're a nutcase' sort of laugh. Might have blown any chance I may have had.

But my chance was still intact.

When Lauren appeared, she smiled and said, 'I'll wait for you.'

Never peed so fast in my life. When I came out, found Sharky was the one doing the talking. Don't know what words he was using, but they clearly weren't working. Lauren was standing as far from him as the hall allowed, arms crossed, face glazed over. Sharky regularly scores zero in reading body language. He has no idea. Decided to come to Lauren's rescue.

'Sharky, haven't you got some homework that needs doing?'

His face crumpled. Wasn't happy about me muscling in, but he'd get over it. Not like he'd invested a ton of time on her. Lauren and I found a small sofa to squidge up on. It was in the dining room, close to the DJ. Could have found somewhere quieter, but the noise had its benefits. Whenever Lauren talked, she'd bring her mouth super-close to my ear. The warmth of her wine-breath sent vibes to every corner of my anatomy. Found out she went to St Bernadette's, an all-girl's school on the other side of town. Liked netball and swimming. Had a younger brother called Eliot, who was in the year below me at Copsem. I told her about me, removing any bad bits. Mentioned Mum, Dad, Poppy and Biscuit. Said I had a group of friends, carefully sidestepping the word 'gang'.

Lauren was truly stunning. Imagined any minute a guy would grab her hand and whisk her away. But the guy and the whisking never happened. A few drinks later found the courage to ask if she wanted to meet up again. She said yes. Found some more courage and kissed her lips for real.

We met again and again and again.

Things might have turned out different if Lauren's dad hadn't lost his job at the council. Family were short of cash. Her mum had to care for Lauren's gran who had dementia. Enter the Silk Elephant Thai Restaurant. Lauren got work there four nights a week, including Friday and Saturday. Four sevenths of the week without her. Sunday became our day, when I'd give my adrenalin a day off and we'd chill. The big hole in my calendar got filled with some slightly deranged guys who shared a passion for misbehaving. Sometimes asked myself why I did it. Wasn't it enough to have a gorgeous girlfriend? Shouldn't I have seen the guys twice a month, instead of twice a week? Couldn't I have found a hobby that kept me out of trouble?

No.

That's not how life works.

Especially my life.

Get the urge to do stuff.

The urge is still there.

Also, I'd been hanging out with the guys for years. Put a lot of hours into building these friendships. Didn't want to knock them down like they meant nothing. Not how loyalty works.

Trudge into the house. Dump the shopping bags on the floor. Put Mum's change and loyalty card on the kitchen table.

'Did you get everything?'

'Yeah.'

'What's the matter?'

Mum knows it takes more than shopping to create this look on my face.

'Lauren was there.'

'Oh, my god,' she says, gripping the edge of the kitchen table.

Mum liked Lauren. Thought she'd be a calming influence on me. Ha. Would take a dozen Laurens to calm me down.

'What did she say?'

'What do you think?'

'What did *you* say?'

'Said I wished it hadn't happened. Stuff like that.'

'You didn't say "stuff like that"?'

Mum clearly thinks I'm the world's biggest idiot.

'No, I didn't.' Fiddle with the toggles of my hoody. 'She cried.'

'Poor Lauren,' says Mum, looking like she might cry too. 'Must be horrendous for her.'

'You mean it's not horrendous for me?'

'I never said that,' snaps Mum. 'It's her brother, for goodness' sake. Think what their life is going to be like for the next… who knows how many years.'

I think about little else.

Stare at the bags on the table. Mum could have saved some money. Not sure I ever want to eat again.

'You're going to have to get used to it, Rory.'

'What?'

'People like Lauren saying things.'

Maybe Mum and Dad could get me a tutor, like Dean, to teach me how to deal with having crap hurled at me.

Mum looks out of the kitchen window as rain begins to spatter against the glass. 'Did she say how Eliot is?'

'Showed me photos.'

Wished I'd never seen them. But it's like the sick stuff you see on social. You don't want to look, but you have to. Your eyes demand it. And once you've seen it, it stays there, stuck in your head, like an axe.

The legs of a kitchen chair let out a sharp screech as Mum's bum makes hard contact.

'This is such a nightmare.'

No, Mum, nightmares stop when the sun comes up. Mine start when the alarm clock goes off. Another day facing up to what I've done. And things I haven't done.

'Did Lauren say anything else?'

'No.'

Decide not to tell her what she said about me paying for what happened. An image of her cousin, Andy, in camouflage gear, flashes in front of me. How would we defend ourselves against a soldier? Build trenches around the house? Put up barbed wire? Buy a tank?

Hear the front door open. Followed by the sound of size six shoes.

The kitchen door opens.

'Hi, sweetheart.'

'Hi, Mummy.'

My sister, Poppy, looking as cute as a kitten video in her Year Seven Copsem uniform. She gets a hug and the sort of smile Mum reserves for her favourite child. She's the opposite of me in every possible way. Mr Must-Try-Harder versus Miss Couldn't-Try-Any-Harder. Poppy's got the genius gene that somehow sidestepped me. She's not only good at sport, speaks Spanish, is up to grade seven piano, she gets report cards so good, reckon she must write them herself.

She's also sensitive.

Which is less good.

Sometimes comes home crying when the questions about her errant brother get too much. Mum and Dad told her to limit time on her phone, to avoid anything stupid spinning around about me. But, like everyone, she's addicted and sees everything.

'Hi, Poppy,' I say, in the breeziest voice I can find.

'Hi, Rory. Have you been out?'

She's spotted I'm wearing a hoody. Never wear one round the house.

'Yeah, got some food.'

'Did you get chocolate brownies?'

'Yeah.'

She grins.

Don't want to tell her who I met by the pet food. That will only kickstart her tear glands. She loves Lauren. They used to make jewellery together. Poppy would try to teach her piano, even though Lauren's fingers weren't up to it.

'You don't look very happy,' says Poppy, staring at me, like some miniature mind-reader.

'Hate shopping.'

'But the shopping's finished.'

Mum and I swap looks but don't swap them fast enough.

'What's going on?' Poppy asks, her eyes swivelling between me and Mum, unsure who to settle on.

I nod at Mum.

'Rory bumped into Lauren at the supermarket.'
'Oh.'
'Yeah, oh,' I repeat.
'What did she say?'
'Stuff.'
Poppy taps her foot, clearly wanting more.
'You still going to see her?'
'You'd better get changed, sweetheart,' said Mum. 'You've got piano practice at five.'
'I want to know.'
Can't stand it any longer.
'I won't be seeing Lauren again.'
'But you saw her today.'
'That was an accident.'

Poppy's face crumples and she flounces off to her room. Wait until her door slams, before heading up to mine. Lie on my bed counting the cracks in the ceiling, imagining they're cracks in my head, letting bad things in.

Yell.

All the tubes coming from him.

Lauren.

Tears falling on to her shopping.

The threat.

You are so going to pay for this.

ELEVEN

'**RORY, CAN YOU** take your headphones off?' shouts Mum.

Tempted to leave them on. If I listen to loud music long enough, might damage my hearing and never have to listen to what people are saying about me.

But that's too stupid.

Even for me.

Turn the music off.

Mum finds a chair in the corner of the room. As far away from me as possible.

'I've noticed you've been spending a lot of time in your room lately.'

'Thought that's what you wanted.'

'Well it's not. I want us all to sit down to a family dinner tonight.'

'Why?'

'To celebrate my son not going to court.'

'Thought you weren't bothered.'

'Well that's where you're wrong. I'm incredibly bothered.'

'What about Dad?'

'He's okay with it.'

'Just okay?'

'Cut him some slack, Rory. We've had a massive shock. None of this is in the parenting handbook.'

If a baby came with a book of instructions wonder what mine would say.

Handle with care.

'Didn't mean to hurt you, Mum.'

'I know.' She gets up and heads for the door. Then stops and turns. 'Rory, you can't change what's happened, you can only change how you behave going forward.' Mum should get a job in pastoral care. 'I need to see that from you.'

'Sure.'

And so that night we play a new game, Ordinary Families. I come downstairs to find Mum's cooked a huge pot of spag bol, with salad and garlic bread. The garlic bread would have done me, my appetite's gone missing. There are no sightings of it. Mum pours herself a large glass of wine. Dad opens a bottle of beer. Poppy has an apple juice. Biscuit waits at the corner of the table, nose in the air, tongue lolling, waiting for anything that comes his way. We sit down to eat, as if everything is normal.

'I want this to be a turning point,' says Dad, as he sips his beer.

'What's that mean?' asks Poppy.

'It means a change in behaviour, attitude.'

'Your dad's right, you need to promise there'll be no more stupidity,' says Mum, staring at me.

'Sure.'

Mum and Dad exchange glances, pleased with the way things are going.

'Does that mean I can have my phone and laptop back?'

More glances at Dad. It's obviously been discussed in depth at one of their board meetings.

'Yes, you can have them back,' says Mum. 'On condition your phone stays on at all times. We need to know where you are.'

I've been tagged by the house police.

'And we are limiting your screen time,' goes Dad. 'Social Media is a cesspit.'

'I'll go shower every time I use it.'

'We want you to knuckle down and get the best GCSE grades you can.'

Without a girlfriend or gang what else is there to do?

'Can I have my phone now?'

'No, you can have it in the morning,' says Dad. 'We don't want you doom scrolling all night. Thought it'd be nice if we watched a movie together.'

Not Dad's best idea. We can never agree on what to watch. Mum likes romantic comedies, Dad likes war documentaries, Poppy likes teen dramas. I like Marvel films. Unless he can find a film about a fun-loving teenage soldier in the Second World War who falls in love with a girl who develops superpowers, none of us is going to be happy.

We let Mum choose and sit down to watch a romantic comedy called *Freeze a Crowd*, about three divorced middle-aged women who go to Norway and get involved with three divorced middle-aged men. I'd normally rather scoop my eyeballs out with a spoon than watch something like this, but I play along. It's part of the corner I'm meant to be turning.

Look at Mum and Dad, squidged on the sofa, nursing their drinks. Poppy, curled up on a bean bag, while our Cavapoo, Biscuit, nestles in her lap. For the first time in a long time seems we're a normal family.

Maybe things are finally getting better.

Bam!

Our front window erupts in a billowing cloud of glass as a brick hurtles through. It smashes our glass coffee table, before thudding into the carpet. I stare at the mess. How can one window make so many pieces? Poppy screams and crawls back up the sofa, as if a bomb's gone off. Biscuit races around the room, barking with all the volume his little body can muster. Mum and Dad leap to their feet, spilling drinks, adding to the mess.

'What on earth...' shouts Mum, wiping wine stains from her jeans.

As Poppy continues to sob, Dad picks up the brick and reads what's written on the side.

Rory is dead.

TWELVE

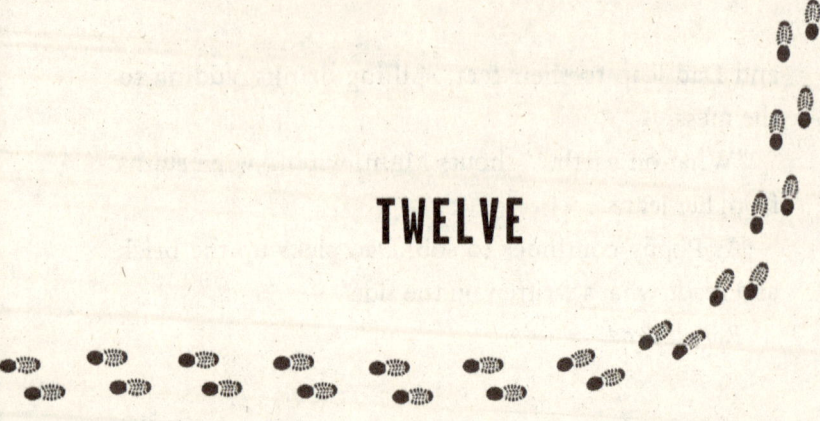

DAD RACES OUT of the front door. I'm a few paces behind. He stands, hands on hips, as he looks up and down the street. My eyes do the same. There's no one about. Whoever threw the brick was probably on a bike or e-scooter. They'll be long gone.

'Who the hell did this?' exclaims Dad, the cold air turning his words into clouds.

My brain runs through the possible suspects. Lauren has to be top of the list. Never put her down as a brick thrower, but strange it arrives the same day I bump into her. And there's her threat: *you are so gonna pay for this*. Could be her cousin, Andy, the soldier. But someone with access to so many weapons would throw something far more dangerous than a brick. Her dad? He's out of work. Maybe he's got nothing better to do than brood all day about what's happened to his son. Then there's her oversized family – grandparents, cousins, uncles, aunts, nephews, nieces. Could be any one of them.

Our next-door neighbour, Brian Harris, appears at his door, his breath coming in machine-gun bursts.

'Heard a terrible noise. What's happened, Alan?'

'Someone threw a brick through our window.'

'Hell's teeth. Why would anyone do that?'

Brian's eyes alight on me. His question is instantly answered. He knows exactly why a brick has been delivered through the window of 25 Yatesbury Avenue.

'Anyone hurt?'

Dad shakes his head.

'Have you got a doorbell camera, Brian?'

'I never saw the need. Such a nice area.'

Till now.

'If you see anything suspicious, let us know.'

'Will do.'

Brian goes back inside. I see the curtains move in the house across the road. A face appears at a window that's still in one piece. This will be the talk of the neighbourhood tomorrow. I've added a sprinkle of spice to their dull existence.

'Come on,' says Dad, putting a hand on my shoulder, ushering me back into the house. He closes the front door and we go into the sitting room. Mum still has her arms wrapped around Poppy, while Biscuit continues to run around as if he's chasing an invisible squirrel.

'Take Poppy to her room,' says Dad.

'She's got no slippers on. There's glass on the floor.'

Dad sighs and goes over to her. She's not a child any more, but he picks her up as though she is and carries her to the door. Mum tiptoes after them. 'And somebody get Biscuit out of here. He'll cut his paws.'

Scoop Biscuit into my arms. Can feel his heart going berserk inside his body. He's in competition with me to see whose can go fastest. Take him into the kitchen and close the door.

Go back to the sitting room.

Laughter erupts.

The three middle-aged men are trying to skate and manage to pull each other over on the ice. Pick up the TV remote and put us all out of our misery.

Mum and Dad return.

'I should have closed the curtains,' she says, staring at the hole where there once was a window.

Dad pulls his phone from his pocket and dials 999. He tells them about the brick, the message, gives them our address and hangs up. Then he turns on me.

'You are going to pay for this.'

Lauren's words. Without the 'so'.

'We'll go half,' says Mum.

'We will not go half. He pays for it. This is his fault.'

Look down at the glass. No idea how much windows cost. Only got eighty quid in my account. But then I don't go out any more.

'I'll clear it up,' I say, getting to my feet.

'No, leave it,' says Mum. 'It's evidence.'

'What, the police gonna fingerprint every tiny shard?'

'I don't know,' she sighs, exasperated. 'I'm no expert.'

Not sure the police will do much. Probably take one look, give us a crime number and go back to the canteen. Need to get out of this room, with the brick and the glass and the atmosphere. Decide against upstairs. Spent way too long up there. Go to the kitchen. Sit at the table, head in my hands, as Biscuit paws at my leg, wanting to play. Thought things would get better over time. But they're only getting worse.

First Lauren.

Now the brick.

So much for a normal family.

THIRTEEN

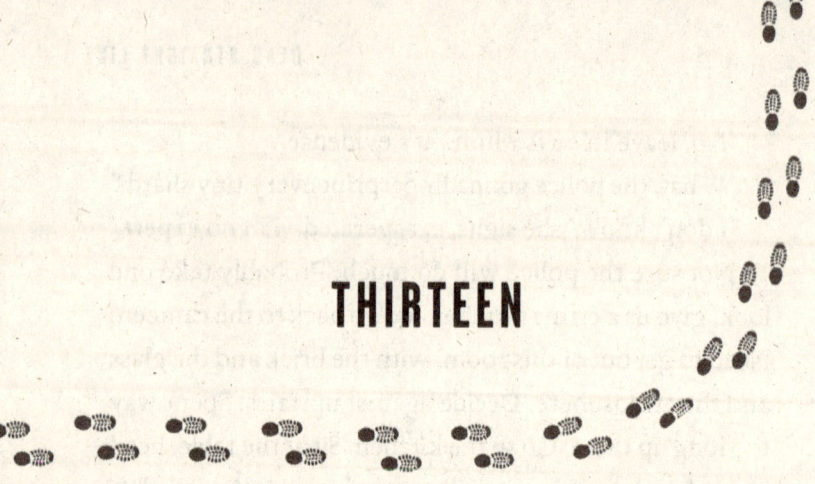

NOT MUCH HAPPENED over the next few days, apart from Poppy having nightmares and crying for no reason, Mum spending more time watching the street than she did the TV, and Dad saving his spite and spittle for me. The police found no witnesses or CCTV footage. They went to speak to Yell's family, but they had an alibi. They'd all gone to see his grandparents who live out of town. Lauren had nothing to do with it. The phantom brick thrower was still out there.

But it isn't the end of the bad news.

The brick didn't just smash the window, it destroyed any chance of getting my phone back. Must be the only teenager in the world without one. Means I still can't find out what's happening. Apple will probably be up to the iPhone 50 by the time I get mine.

I'm sulking on the sofa one night when my parents come and sit either side of me.

I'm in a Mum-and-Dad sandwich.

'We've got some news,' says Mum.

'About your education.'

'We've found a new school for you.'

'Hayford Free,' says Dad.

Wish only one of them would speak. My neck's hurting from all the swivelling.

'We've spoken to the headteacher, Mrs Bellingham.'

'We told her what you did.'

'You said I didn't push him.'

'We didn't get into that.'

'Why not?'

'We were there to talk about your future.'

'What future?'

'Rory, please.'

'She's okay about recruiting a juvenile delinquent?' I ask.

Mum sighs out an entire lungful of breath.

'We told her you show a lot of promise.'

Not the only liar in the house.

'What do you think?' says Mum, giving me a gentle nudge.

'Hayford is miles away.'

Dad kicks at a dog toy on the floor. 'Is that all you've got to say?'

Shrug.

'They've got a good academic record.'

'I'll soon change that.'

'Oh, for crying out loud, Rory. Mrs Bellingham is giving you a great opportunity here. Take it.'

Stare through our brand-new window, wondering how long it will last.

'Rory, can you be gracious for once.'

'Gracious for what? My friends are all at Copsem. I don't know anyone there.'

'You soon will. You're very sociable.'

'Look where that's got me.'

'It'll give you a fresh start,' says Dad.

My parents have got an answer for everything. Maybe they should sit my GCSEs.

Mum takes my hand. I take it back again.

'Good can come from bad,' she says.

That does it.

Time for the Mum-and-Dad sandwich to lose its filling.

Leap from the sofa and stomp upstairs to my room. My back finds the mattress. My eyes find the ceiling. I don't want to go to this stupid school with a load of nerdy high achievers I don't know. All I want right now is to get out of this house. Apart from my family, the only people I've spoken to these last few weeks are Lauren and the police. I need to know what's going on.

But who to ask?

One name jumps to the front of the queue.

Sharky.

Known him since we wore ties we couldn't tie and laces we struggled to lace. Seeing as exams are coming up, his parents have started taking his studies seriously. Like Dean, he goes to a maths tutor on a Tuesday night. Which happens to be tonight. Remember his session finishes at 9.30 p.m. Look at my bedside alarm. 8.42 p.m. Still time for me to meet him before he gets home.

Slight problem.

Mum and Dad have barred me from going out at night.

But rules and me aren't exactly friends.

Wait till 9 p.m., pull on my hoody and slowly open the bedroom window. Have that feeling I get every time we play our games. I shouldn't be doing this. And every time I do.

Climb out of the window, on to the sloping roof, then clamber down the drainpipe and drop to the patio in the back garden. All with the maximum amount of silence. There's a gap in the curtains. Peep in. Mum and Dad are slumped on the sofa, sedated by whatever's on TV.

Hurry across the lawn, over the fence and into the alley behind our house. Pull my hoody up, keep my head down and make my way towards Sharky's. Even though I stick to the paths, my nerves jangle like wind chimes in a storm. Mum and Dad would kill me if they knew.

Reach Sharky's street. Don't want to be seen loitering outside his front door, so I wait opposite his house, under a broken streetlight, praying his mum hasn't gone to pick him up. The prayer works. A few minutes later, I spot him walking up the street, brain full of algorithms. Need to head him off before he reaches his house.

Rush over the road.

'Sharky,' I say, with as much volume as I dare.

He looks up. And smiles. But it disappears in an instant, as if someone's flicked his de-smile switch.

'R-Rory,' he stutters. 'What are you doing here?'

'Talking to you.'

Hold out my hand. A peace offering. He looks about, as if shaking hands is socially unacceptable round here.

'I washed it.'

He finally gives it a quick squeeze.

Got Sharky to do some pretty crazy stuff over the years, but never seen him look as nervous as he does now.

'Chill, man. It's only me.'

'Yeah,' he goes, as if he's about to be jumped.

'How's things?' I ask, trying to keep it light.

'Cool.'

'What's up, man. English become your second language?'

'Not meant to be in contact with you.'

'I did the contacting.'

Sharky doesn't look convinced.

'Who said you couldn't get in touch?'

'Mum.'

'Well, she's not here, is she? You're sixteen, Sharky. You can make your own mind up.'

'Things have changed.'

Too right.

'How's Yell?'

'Not back at school yet. Having rehab. The school are putting in ramps.'

'Seen much of the guys?'

''Course I have, we're in the same class.'

'What's everyone saying... about me?'

His Adam's apple bobs as he swallows. 'That it was your game. That you made him do it. That you pushed him.'

'Everyone saying that?'

Sharky nods.

'Even though there's no evidence?'

Sharky fiddles with the zip on his jacket. 'We were all there the night you asked him, Rory. We heard what you said. "You have to do it, Yell. It's the law round these parts."'

'I didn't make him.'

'Sounded like it to us.'

Can't believe what Sharky's saying.

'Do you honestly think I pushed him?'

'I need to get home, Rory.'

Sharky's a friend, but even friendships have their limits. I grab him by the collar of his coat, tightening it around his neck and back him into a wall. Don't want to have to get violent but can't think of another way to squeeze words out of him. 'You haven't answered my question.'

'It's difficult.'

'No, it's not. Do you believe Yell or me?'

Spot a woman coming down the street. Let go of Sharky's collar but block him against the wall. Don't want him running off before I've got what I came for. I wait for her heels to click away into nothingness.

'Well?'

'You pushed me off Clinker's Bridge first time we climbed up there. You were so impatient.'

'You're saying 'cos I pushed you into a river I pushed Yell off a roof?'

His silence speaks volumes.

'You believe Yell, and not me?'

'I don't want any trouble,' mumbles Sharky.

'Bit late for that. Trouble's already here, and I'm the one up to my neck in it.'

Sharky could have helped me. He could have said Yell went along with the game, that it was an accident, that he jumped. But he's done the opposite. Now everyone believes him. Not me.

'I'm looking for a bit of support, Sharky.'

Judging from his face, I'm not about to get any. Sharky loosens the collar I've tightened around his neck. It does nothing for his vocal chords. He uses his right to remain silent, looking down the street, as if I'm not there.

'Sharky, have you any idea what this is doing to me?'

'Course he doesn't. Sharky has no imagination.

Maybe I can get to the truth another way.

'Someone threw a brick through our front window.'

'Yeah?' he nods, as if it's no different to a birthday card through your letterbox.

'They wrote *Rory is dead* on the side.'

Sharky's eyes swivel this way and that, as if a phantom brick thrower might appear any second and start hurling them at us.

'Mum'll wonder where I am,' he mutters.

After Dead Straight Line reckon she keeps tabs on him. Probably on Life360 now wondering why he's suddenly stopped metres from their front door.

'Maybe we could meet up some time. Have a proper talk. Using proper sentences and stuff.'

'Best if we don't, Rory.'

Could not be more disappointed in him.

'You'd better go. Don't want to keep Mummy waiting.'

Sharky hurries away without so much as a goodbye. Was this really the guy I hung out with since primary school? Do all those years count for nothing? I watch him scurry up his path and through the front door.

Should have stayed in. The guy I thought I could trust, thinks I'm to blame for what happened. I know why he's done it. Self-preservation. Needs to distance himself from me and that night. He wants to make out that I ran everything, like some gangster boss. Wants to turn him and Dean and Mad and Barny into innocent bystanders.

Head home, anger stoking my heart.

Go along the alley behind our house, clear the garden fence, climb the drainpipe and clamber through my open bedroom window.

The second I drop to the floor, I'm blinded by a hundred-watt bulb. Dad, stands there, face flushed, fists balled.

'Where the hell have you been?'

FOURTEEN

NOW IS NOT the time for smart-arse answers.

'Went to see Sharky.'

'You absolute clown,' screams Dad.

'Alan, Poppy's trying to sleep,' whispers Mum, as she grips the frame of my bedroom door.

Dad clearly isn't bothered, as he continues to rant. 'We told him to stay in, and what's the first thing he does? Climbs through the bedroom window like some burglar. Does he not listen to anything we say?'

No.

'When did you two arrange to meet?' asks Mum softly.

'It was my idea to see him. Sharky doesn't do ideas.'

'You're an absolute disgrace,' roars Dad.

I've had enough. My blood soars past simmer and starts to boil. Dad doesn't have a monopoly on anger.

'Yes, I'm sorry I involved Yell in Dead Straight Line and for what happened to him, but I don't deserve this…

you two treating me like a convicted criminal. Why won't you trust me?'

'We have always trusted you, Rory,' says Mum. 'And look where it's got us. From now on, you're going to have to earn our trust. It comes with the right behaviour.'

'And what about your behaviour? I came up with a game, that's all, and I've been punished as if I've committed a serious crime. I've lost my girlfriend, my school, my friends. I no longer have a phone or a social life or any life for that matter. That's why I decided to meet Sharky tonight. I wanted to talk to someone other than you two. Need to find out what he and the rest of the guys think. And, guess what, they think I pushed Yell, so you're in good company. Do you know what else – he said he never wants to see me again. I thought he was my best friend.'

Don't know if it's my outburst, or seeing Sharky, or everything else that's gone on, but I can't hold it together. Sit down on the bed, tears turning Mum and Dad blurry.

'We'll talk about it in the morning,' says Dad, as he retreats towards the door.

'Check to see Poppy's okay,' says Mum.

Yeah, make sure your daughter is fine.

A bedspring squeaks as Mum sits next to me. Feel a gentle hand on my head. 'I know how tough this is for you, Rory, but there will be light at the end of the tunnel.'

Feels like there's tunnel at the end of the tunnel.

'We can get through this. It's going to take time, but we can do it. Get some sleep.' She kisses me on the cheek and turns off the bedroom light.

I climb into bed fully clothed and go in search of nightmares.

Wake the next morning to find my sheets have been on the spin cycle. Check my bedside clock. It's 10.37 a.m. Been in bed for hours. Feel I've slept for seconds. Consider staying here all day. That would make Mum and Dad happy. Can't get up to any mischief glued to a mattress. But the idea is way too boring.

Get showered and go downstairs. Pray Dad's not working from home today. What were his last words? *We'll talk about it in the morning.*

No, Dad, let's not.

Mum's sitting at the kitchen table reading a book. She slams it shut and puts it face down. Not before I glimpse the title. *Inside the Teenage Brain*.

Good luck with that.

'Morning, Rory,' she says, trying not to blush.

'Where's Dad?'

'Gone to work.' Mum folds her arms and looks at me. 'This has to stop, Rory.'

'What, me coming down for breakfast?'

'Can you park the stupid remarks for one second, please?'

I steer my stupidity into a parking space and turn off the engine.

'I'm talking about what happened last night. You jumping out of your window.'

'How else am I meant to get out of the house?'

'The front door, like a normal person. I don't want you living in this world of sneaky behaviour, as if you're a spy or something. I want us all to be happy.'

Happy would mean turning the clock back to the night everything went wrong. Remember walking up to Soapy Suds, feeling excited, energised, alive. Now I feel like a phone on one per cent power, waiting to die.

'You start your new school next week. Look at it as a new chapter.'

More like the end of a book. One where everyone dies. Horribly.

Mum reads my mind.

'Please, Rory. Give it a chance. I know how hard this is, but you've got to try to make the most of it.'

Run my fingers through my hair. 'None of this is… fair.'

Mum's face darkens. 'Your grandad getting dementia wasn't fair either. It wasn't fair on any of us. It happened all the same. Gran had to live with it. I had to live with it. And he had to die with it.' Mum looks off as the memory makes her lips wobble. 'And it's not fair what happened to Eliot.'

He gatecrashes my brain. Everything was going fine for Yell. Then I happened. Now he's going to have to adjust to a whole load of things he's never had to deal with before. At the age of fifteen. Guess that's the definition of unfair.

'I'll try, Mum.'

Mum gets up and gives me a hug. But the hug's over before it's begun.

'I don't believe it,' she exclaims.

'What?'

Mum rushes to the kitchen window.

'The washing I put on the line this morning. It's gone.'

FIFTEEN

'**CHARLIE, YOU DIDN'T** spell-check your story, did you?'

'No, Mrs Shields.'

Charlie Townsend, a big guy with the makings of a beard, sits staring at his desk as if he's searching for woodworm.

'Look at me when I'm talking to you.' Charlie lifts his head slowly, as if it weighs a hundred tons. 'You wrote,' says Mrs Shields, looking at a piece of paper, 'the boy was curled in a fecal position.' Sniggers echo around the class. 'It's foetal position, as in a foetus, curled up inside a mother's womb. Fecal is body waste.'

So much for this place being academic.

'You could be curled up like a turd,' says Charlie hopefully.

The snigger count goes up.

'Yes, you could, but not sure that will go down well with the examiners.'

Welcome to my new school. I've been at Hayford Free two weeks now. Could have been better. Could have been worse. Won't forget my first day. Mum said no one would be bothered about what I'd done. How wrong can you be? I was all they were bothered about.

Is it true he fell from the sixth floor?
Did you give him CPR?
How come you're not in prison?

Thankfully, the questions died off, as students grew bored with my answers, which were as dull as I could make them.

The new school coincided with getting my phone back. Not sure I should have been in such a hurry. The incident with Yell has spread like a pandemic, along with the usual errors, fakery and exaggerations, as if Charlie Townsend had written them all. Seems the hate mob has been working an extra shift, piling in with whatever bile they can spew. But worse than what was being said, was what wasn't being said. Not a single word, thumbs up or smiley face from Mad, Sharky, Dean or Barny. Zilch. I know their parents want them to have nothing to do with me but thought one of them might have had the guts to get their thumb out and send a message.

I'm sick of being singled out for something I didn't even do. I'm more than that.

Stare out of the class window. Don't want to be in school. I want to be outside, doing stuff that doesn't involve angles or equations or dead kings and queens or elements or pronouns or sand-dunes or anything else they try to load your head with. When I've done my GCSEs, I'm leaving. Me and school don't get along. We've tried, but we're incompatible. Not even on speaking terms. Best we go our separate ways.

Mum and Dad will hate me for quitting. To add to the pile of other things they hate me for. The English lesson trundles on, the way they do, and the bell finally goes. Gather my books and head for the door at glacial speed. Which seems appropriate. My next lesson is geography with Mrs Harding.

'Rory,' says Mrs Shields.

'Yeah.'

'Stay behind for a second.'

Heads turn. They want to know why I've been held back. What they can't find, they'll make up. Without gossip, reckon most kids in Year Eleven would die. It's the fuel that keeps them going. A group of girls hangs around the door, ears on high alert.

'Out,' shouts Mrs Shields.

A collective groan bursts from four sets of lips. The girls troop out. Mrs Shields waits until the last of them has left before closing the door.

'Take a seat.'

I sit down and cross my arms.

'How are things?'

Mrs Shields isn't just my English teacher, she's also my year tutor.

'Brilliant.'

Hopefully, that will put a stop to her questions. Studying U-shaped valleys is preferable to another how's-it-going chat.

'You don't seem brilliant.'

Decide to give her a bit of news that might shut her down.

'Someone stole our clothes.'

'What?'

'Yeah, they nicked our clothes from the washing line in our garden.' Mrs Shields slaps her hand to her mouth. 'They turned up on our front lawn a few days later... slashed to pieces. They'd cut the legs off my jeans. Think they were trying to send a message.'

'Oh, that's terrible.'

'Probably the same person or people who threw a brick through our front window.'

Mrs Shields looks shocked, aghast, stunned, appalled, dismayed. Thanks, Thesaurus.

'Did you see who it was?'

'No.'

Mrs Shields shakes her head as if she's got water trapped in her ear. 'Why would anyone do such a horrible thing?'

'Because they believe I pushed Eliot Hollings, the guy from Copsem High, off a roof. Seeing as I'm not going to court, decided to carry out their own vendetta.'

'I'm sorry, Rory.' Mrs Shields composes herself. 'I know it's been tough for you, but we're here to help. If there's anything we can do, please ask.'

'Sure.'

I get up.

'I haven't finished yet.'

Sit back down.

'There's something I'd like to talk to you about. As you know, Hayford Free has a history of helping people less fortunate than ourselves.'

'There are people less fortunate than me?'

'Believe it or not, Rory, yes. We like to give back.'

Not sure I've got anything to give, unless you include sarcasm.

'You're a good reader.'

'Not as good as my sister.'

'We're not talking about her. I was impressed with the way you read that extract from Dickens.'

It was the best of times, it was the worst of times.

Make your mind up, Dickens.

'For the last few years we've been running a project called New Chapters. It involves Mannings Care Home near the Yaxton Estate. Do you know it?'

Nod.

Mad and I did Dead Straight Line through their gardens a few months ago. Mad fell into an ornamental pond. Think he squashed a carp.

'We invite students to go to the home to read to elderly residents.'

'Why can't they read themselves?'

'Some of them can't. Poor eyesight. Dyslexia. Poor concentration. Others can read but enjoy the company. You can earn extra house points.'

We've got four houses at Hayford: Darwin, Austen, Gandhi and Curie. My house is Darwin, named after the bloke who discovered evolution. Trying to win points for people who've been dead hundreds of years. What is the purpose of that?

'Darwin is lagging behind this year.'

'Poor old Darwin.'

Mrs Shields looks on the brink of getting annoyed, but reins it in. 'You can help, Rory. There's a hundred points for every student who takes part.'

'Wow.'

'Less of that, please. Why not give it some thought.'

'I have. I'm not doing it.'

Get to my feet and head for the door.

Glaciers here I come.

SIXTEEN

I'M SITTING IN a classroom with five other students. All girls.

'So glad you've agreed to join us, Rory,' says Mrs Shields.

'Anything to help the oldies.'

'Can you not call them that, please.'

'Coffin dodgers?'

'Absolutely not.'

'Senior citizens.'

'Thank you.'

A week ago, I was dead against taking part in Hayford's reading initiative. Rather watch *Freeze a Crowd*. So why the change of heart? It had nothing to do with helping senior citizens or pleasing Mrs Shields or precious house points for Charles Darwin. It had everything to do with me.

Reason one. I've got nothing to do. Yes, I have to study, but as I plan to leave school at the end of the year, no point cramming my brain with crap I'll never need.

Be like filling your fridge with stones or topping up your petrol tank with soda.

Reason two. I need to get out of the house. Mum and Dad now make me spend evenings with them. Must think if I'm left alone in my room with my phone, I'll do something stupid, like get in touch with North Korea and start World War III. Instead, I sit on the sofa watching property programmes, with house hunters going teary-eyed over ceilings and south-facing gardens. The day I start enjoying them, I'll personally ask Lauren's cousin to come around and kill me.

Reason three. The tension in our house is too much. Since the brick through the window and the shredded clothes, Mum and Dad have been on super-high alert, like wildebeest looking out for lions. Dad watches TV with a baseball bat next to the sofa, forever checking his phone to see what's happening outside on our doorbell camera. Mum is on tablets and has taken up knitting to calm her nerves. Poppy has meltdowns which happen when you least expect them. Even Biscuit is jumpy, barking at things that aren't the slightest bit bark-worthy.

When I told Mum she was so delighted, she did a little jig around the kitchen.

Oh, that's such a positive, empathetic thing to do, Rory.

Yay, what a hero. Give me a medal.

*

The New Chapters night arrives.

A minibus turns up at school and we climb in. Manage to grab a seat on my own at the back. For once, I want to be ignored.

Doesn't last long.

Eden, a girl in my class, plonks herself next to me. She looks familiar but can't picture where I've seen her.

'Have you done this before?' she asks.

'What, travelled in a minibus?'

'No, read for older people.'

'Read the TV guide for my gran once when she lost her glasses. So yeah, guess I have.'

'It's very rewarding.'

'They give you money?'

'No, it's good for your soul,' interjects Mrs Shields, who has her ears tuned into me.

Decide to keep my mouth clamped for the rest of the journey.

We reach the care home and follow Mrs Shields inside. The place smells of cleaning fluid. Apart from the staff, everyone looks about a million years old. We get taken to an office, where a middle-aged woman with dyed blonde hair is sitting behind a desk. She gets up and gives Mrs Shields a hug.

'Hello, Rachel,' says the woman.

'Hello, Flora.'

She releases Mrs Shields and turns her gaze to me. 'See we've got a new addition to the group.'

'Yes, this is Rory.'

'Rory the story,' says Eden.

Laughs from the girls.

None from the only boy in the room.

'Welcome, Rory. I'm Flora York, manager of Mannings Care Home.'

'Cool.'

'Okay, you stay here, Rory, with me and Mrs York,' says Mrs Shields. 'The girls can go and see the residents.'

Mrs York waits until they've left before closing the door.

'Take a seat, Rory.'

A seat is taken.

'So glad we finally have a young man to come and read for us.'

'I'll do anything for house points.'

'Pardon?'

'Nothing, Flora,' says Mrs Shields. 'One of Rory's little jokes.'

Thinking this was in fact funny, Mrs York gives a small giggle. She then goes over to her desk and opens a file.

'We've thought long and hard about who you can read for, Rory, and after much deliberation we'd like to pair you with Tanker.'

What sort of stupid name's that?

'He's a decent chap,' says Mrs York. 'But can get a bit irascible. Do you know…?'

'Yes, Rory knows what irascible means,' says Mrs Shields.

Even though I don't. Google it later.

'Tanker's got a good heart but can be a bit crotchety. He's a character. Had a tough life. Are you up for meeting him?'

'Sure.'

'Thanks to donations we've got a reasonable library here at Mannings – thrillers, romance, comedies, biographies. You can ask Tanker what he'd like to read. Shall we go to meet him?'

'Yeah.'

Mrs Shields and I follow Mrs York through reception to the lift where she presses the up button.

'Mannings is split into two,' she says. 'The ground and lower ground floors house our residents with dementia. The first and second floors have those yet to show signs of cognitive decline.'

'Why do you keep them apart?'

'Some of our guests with dementia need extra help.'

I remember Grandad near the end. Got angry over nothing at all. Gran and Mum would come back crying.

The lift reaches the second floor. Follow Mrs York down a brightly lit corridor to room twenty-two. The sign on the door says *Tanker*.

Mrs York knocks.

'Come in,' booms a voice.

She opens the door. There, sitting in bed wearing tartan pyjamas, is Tanker – a giant of a man with glasses, a big grey beard and a mass of tangled hair.

'Evening, Tanker, this is Rory.'

'What's he deein here?' says Tanker in a Geordie accent as thick as mud.

'He's here to read for you.'

'What's he ganna read, me gas meter?'

'No, a book, magazine article, whatever you want.'

'Mebes he could read me palm, tell iz when I'm gonna pop me clogs, so I can start packin'.'

I'm going to need an interpreter.

'Rory is in Year Eleven at Hayford Free.'

'And I'm in Year 278 at Mannings Prison Camp.'

Mrs York gives another of her forced laughs.

'Tanker has some books on his shelf,' she says. 'There are more in the library along the corridor. I'm sure you'll find something he'd like to hear. Shall we leave you to it?'

'Aye,' goes Tanker.

'If you need anything, Rory, the internal phone is there,' says Mrs York. 'Simply press one.'

'Good luck, Rory,' says Mrs Shields, touching my arm.

They leave the room and close the door. This is beyond weird. Me reading stories to an old bloke that looks like Santa and who speaks a language that makes my ears ache. Maybe watching property programmes isn't such a bad idea after all.

'Grab a seat young un,' says Tanker.

There's a comfy-looking chair next to his bed. I drop myself into it. Look around the room. There's not a whole lot of looking to be done. A radio. Small wardrobe. Chest of drawers. A photo. Couple of books.

Then I spot something in the corner.

My mouth goes dry.

A wheelchair.

SEVENTEEN

'YOU'VE GOT A wheelchair?'

'Aye, asked for a company car but they give iz this instead. Not exactly fast, but dead friendly to the planet, nee petrol, nee diesel, nee fumes. All you dee is push. If it wasn't for me chariot would take iz boot a week to get to the netty.'

'Netty?'

'Bog, toilet, crap-house, loo – take your pick.' Continue to stare at the wheelchair. 'What's the marra, look like you've seen a ghost?'

'Wasn't expecting to see a wheelchair.'

'Plenty roond here, man. Get traffic jams at mealtimes. Geriatric gridlock.'

'What happened to you?'

Tanker scrabbles with his beard, as if the answer's hidden in there somewhere. 'Used to be in the army; parachute regiment. But wasn't a missile that took me leg off, was a sausage roll.'

'Sausage roll?'

'Aye, along with crisps, beer, pizzas, chocolate, doughnuts, burgers. Got type 2 diabetes. Had me leg amputated.'

'You lost your leg to junk food?'

'Aye, shoulda known berra. But used to comfort eat, see. Daft way to medicate, fillin' your chops with junk food, but couldn't stop mesel. If I was feelin' doon, I'd fill mesel up.'

No idea food could do that to you.

'Had a blister one week. Ignored it, as you dee. Next week they lopped me leg off.'

'Just 'cos of a blister?'

'Aye, got infected. That's what happens when you knacker your body, man. Needed to lose some weight, but not me whole leg.'

'When did it happen?'

'Aboot two year ago.'

Do Geordies not like plurals?

'On me seventy-eighth birthday. Most people get cake. I got surgery.'

'Is that why you came here?'

Tanker looks out of the window at the pond Mad fell in. 'Aye, me place wasn't built for a wheelchair. Doors too narrow. Too many steps. Too many corners. I was a roond peg in a square hoose. They'd need to knock it doon and start again, and the council haven't the money for that, so they put me in here. Didn't wanna leave but nee alternative.'

'Your other leg's okay?'

Tanker laughed. 'Na. Nee strength in it, like a chicken leg with nee chicken on it. Cannit even get aboot on crutches. The prison guards have to hoik me into that thing.'

Thoughts spin to Yell; being helped into his chair, his family having to take on a job they never expected. Or wanted.

'What's the marra? Look like you found a quid and lost a fiver.'

The wheelchair has messed with my speech. Can't think what to say.

Finally dredge something up.

'Do your family visit?'

'Na.'

'What about friends?'

'Na.'

'Why not?'

'Who are you, the Gestapo? Got nee family or friends, right,' snaps Tanker. 'Just shut it with the questions.'

Only been here a couple of minutes and already hacked him off. Probably get kicked out. Zero points for Darwin.

'Tell iz aboot ye?'

'Nothing to say.'

'Must be somethin'.'

'Isn't.'

'Well, this is gonna make for an exhilaratin' visit. Ninety minutes of silence. Ye might as well read me a bedtime story.'

Go over to his bookshelf and look for a book. Find one he might like. *Great Tank Battles of the World*. The book is a thick one. Could take me until Christmas to get through it. I start on the first chapter. The Battle of Cambrai in 1917. Didn't even know tanks were around in the First World War. The facts are more interesting than I imagined. I get to the bit when the British Mark IV tanks break through German lines, when I hear the sound of heavy breathing to my left.

Tanker has flopped to one side on his pillow.

He's fast asleep.

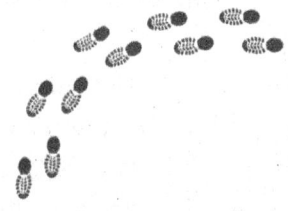

EIGHTEEN

COME OUT OF the lift. Mrs Shields is sitting in reception, reading her Kindle.

'You've finished early,' she says, looking at her watch.

'He fell asleep. In the middle of a tank battle.'

'Elderly people need their rest.'

'Maybe I've got a boring voice.'

'That's not true. Did you and Tanker get on?'

'Not really.'

'Why not?'

'He wouldn't tell me about his family, and I wouldn't tell him about mine.'

'You've got to give people a chance,' she says.

'What, like everyone gave me a chance?'

She has no reply to that.

'We've got nothing in common.'

'You will have. You just have to find it.'

Not sure I can be bothered. There's a sixty-four-year gap between me and him. What's the point in filling it?

'You talk to your grandparents.'

'They're different.'

'Why?'

'We're related. I can't avoid them.'

'But I bet they have some fascinating stories to tell.'

'Sometimes.'

'And I'm sure Tanker will have some amazing things to tell you.'

Already told me one amazing thing about his leg. Doubt he's got any more stories left.

'Anyway, I'm proud of you for coming tonight, Rory.'

Don't know what she's proud about. Read a few pages about tanks to a guy and sent him to sleep. Hardly worth a house point.

Mrs Shields goes back to her book. I go back to my phone to see if everyone still hates me. Nothing's changed on that front.

Eventually the girls appear. They're laughing and smiling. Obviously found the positive experience I missed. We make our way to the minibus. Want the back row, but two girls have already nabbed it. Shuffle into a window seat. No sooner have I sat down than I feel a puffer jacket make soft contact with mine.

'Hiya.'

Eden again.

'Hi.'

Seen her around. At Hayford Free the girls move in shoals. But unlike the fish you see on reefs, their favourite colour is black. Black shoes, black tights, black skirts, black puffer jackets, black eyeliner and, if you say the wrong thing, black looks. Eden even has black hair. She's attractive. Not that I've given anyone much eyeball time. Since Lauren.

'How did Rory the Story get on?'

Wish she'd stop saying that. Wasn't funny the first time.

'Okay.'

'Who were you reading for?' she asks.

'Old guy, ex-army. He's broad Geordie. Bordering on unintelligible. Should come with subtitles.'

'What book did you read?'

'*Great Tank Battles of the World*.'

'Nice. Let's hope it has a happy ending.'

'What about you?' I ask.

'*Pride and Prejudice*.'

It's on our GCSE syllabus. About time I read it. Properly.

'Who do you read for?'

'A sweet lady called Emily. She's ninety-two. Had an amazing life. She used to be a mountain climber. Climbed the Matterhorn in her twenties, Mont Blanc when she was in her seventies. Imagine the risks she must have taken.'

My mind flips to Yell. Scared of being three metres off the ground. I wonder what he's doing now. Probably staring out of his bedroom window, wishing I was dead.

'Are you coming back next week?' asks Eden, giving me a gentle nudge.

'Doubt it,' I say, wiping condensation off the window. 'Don't care much for care homes.'

'Why not?'

'Probably end up in one myself someday. Why go before you have to?'

'Think about the pleasure you bring to people.'

'Not sure I brought much. Tanker fell asleep halfway through a battle. Don't think he'll be begging me to come back.'

'*I'd* like you to come back.'

Is Eden hitting on me? Heard about girls who go mad for bad, like a heat-seeking drone hovering over guys who break the rules. Perhaps she's doing it for a bet. Some guys do that. Ask out the least fit girl, then dump her at the last minute. Laughs come in strange packages.

'There's a party this weekend,' she says. 'Would you like to go?'

'Who with?'

'Emily Ashtead, the ninety-two-year-old mountaineer.' She raises her eyebrows. 'Me, silly.'

My body is keen. My mind isn't. The timing is all wrong. Way too soon after what's gone on, brain mashed up by Yell and Lauren, my so-called friends and everything at home. Bad experiences can do that to you. Like the time at Mad's house, when I downed too many whiskys and half my insides went down the toilet. Haven't touched a drop since.

Dating's like drinking. If you go for it too hard, there's a price to pay.

'What are you thinking?'

Nothing you want to hear.

The window steams up again. Eden leans across and draws a smiley face in the condensation.

'You've no idea what I'm like.'

'And that's where you're wrong, Rory.'

NINETEEN

'**WHAT HAVE YOU** heard?' I ask, hands gripping the seat.

'The rumours about what happened with you and that boy,' she says, our puffer jackets getting close and personal. 'But I don't believe them. Prefer to take people as I find them.'

'And how do you find me?' I whisper, trying to keep our conversation away from the other Hayford girls.

'Cool.'

Long time since anyone described me as that.

'What about me?' she asks.

The more I think about Eden, the better she gets. Those hazel-coloured eyes. Those lips. That mischievous smile. But need to be careful with the words I use. The right ones are fireworks. The wrong ones are explosives.

'You're, you're... ' – *think Rory, think* – '... intriguing.'

'Is that even a compliment?'

'It's not a criticism.'

'Thanks for the non-criticism.'

My words have blown it.

Or perhaps not.

She gives me a nudge.

'I like intriguing.'

I nudge her back. Our puffer jackets getting to know each other.

'When we go to the party,' she says, 'you can discover how intriguing I can be.'

The more I think about my word, the better it gets. Intriguing sums up Eden. Find her strangely fascinating. Why is she so keen on me? Why can't I shake off the feeling that I've seen her somewhere before? And more to the point, where will it end?

Only one way to find out.

'Okay, I'll go to the party.'

'That was the right answer.'

Tell Mum when I get home.

'You don't think it's too soon?' she asks, frown lines furrowing her brow.

Not the response I was expecting.

'What's time got to do with it?'

'People might say it's too early. What with Eliot and Lauren.'

'So, I'm meant to lock myself away for the next sixty years.'

'I didn't say that. People will judge you. They'll judge her.'

'Let them. It's nice to have one person in my life who likes me.'

'We love you, Rory.'

Funny way of showing it.

'Have you spoken to her about...'

'Yes.'

Even though it's more of a no. Eden knows about Yell but I haven't told her what's been happening to our family. Don't want to scare her off before we've even said hello.

'I want you to be careful.'

But Mum isn't me. She's the type to check twenty times before crossing the road. And if I say no to Eden now, how long before I find someone else who finds me cool. I could be Tanker's age before that happens. Need to get on with my life.

And here I am on Saturday night. Getting on with it.

Search the wardrobe for my favourite lucky blue shirt, the one I wore on my first proper date with Lauren. Then I remember, the shirt's luck ran out. It was diced into a hundred pieces by our hater. I put on my second favourite – a green shirt with white trim that I wore to Barny's sixteenth. Pull on some grey trousers that haven't seen legs in months. Find some boots in urgent need of polish and finish off with the leather jacket Mum and Dad got me for Christmas.

Head downstairs.

'You look smart,' says Mum, eyeing me up and down.

'Thanks.'

'But your boots could do with polishing.'

'With a face like this, why would anyone look at my feet?'

She laughs and gives me a hug. 'Be safe. And keep your phone on.'

Catch the bus to the high street. Eden is waiting by the estate agents, as we'd arranged. Black has been dropped from her colour palette. She's wearing a red jacket, blue dress, silver boots. Nothing like the ninja I see in school. She's gazing into the window at the posh houses.

'See anything you fancy?'

'Not until now,' she says. Eden goes on tiptoes and kisses me on the cheek.

'You look… nice,' I say. 'Nice and… intriguing.'

She laughs, puts her arm through mine and we walk down the street. Feels good. For a second. Then a thought smacks me in the face. The last time I walked down this road I was with Yell.

'What are you thinking?' asks Eden, who's noticed my lack of conversation.

'Wondering whose party we're going to.'

'Sadie Mitchell. It's her seventeenth.'

Stop dead in my tracks.

'Sadie? Why didn't you tell me?'

'What difference does it make?'

'She goes to Copsem High.'

'So?'

'That's my old school. There'll be people I know.'

'Rory, get a grip. If you go to the cinema, the park, the supermarket, there'll be people from Copsem.'

'But this is a birthday party. It'll be packed full of them.' Run my fingers through my hair. 'How do you know Sadie?'

'Friend of a friend.'

'Does she know I'm coming?'

'No. She said I could bring someone.'

Have no idea what Sadie feels about me, but her party's not the place to find out. It will be full to the attic of people glad I got thrown out of school.

'They'll be over it by now.'

Some, maybe.

'Who could hate you?'

'How long have you got?'

Eden takes my hand and laces her fingers through mine. 'We have to go. Told Sadie I was coming. I've got a present for her. If the atmosphere turns nasty, we leave.'

Should have gone to a movie.

We head towards Sadie's house, but my pace slackens. In no hurry to get there. Eden chats all the way, without a care in the world. A few streets later, the deep repetitive boom of bass tells me we've nearly reached our destination. There are party balloons tied to the gatepost. The house looks familiar. Think me and Barny went through their back garden a few months ago.

I stop at the gate.

'Come on, it'll be fine,' says Eden. 'They'll be so drunk they won't even recognise you.'

She drags me towards the house. A few kids are vaping by the front door. We walk through their pungent cloud into the hall. Seems weird to be entering by the front door. Peer into the lounge where a middle-aged DJ in a cowboy hat is blasting out music at a level that could rearrange your internal organs. See a couple I recognise, but they're too busy locking lips to pay any attention to me.

'Let's find the kitchen,' Eden shouts.

It's quieter in here.

Eden takes out a present and card and leaves them on a pile with other offerings.

'What's this?' she says, peering into a large glass bowl that contains something hideous looking.

'Wallpaper paste?'

'Hmm, my favourite,' says Eden, as she grabs a couple of paper cups, tops them up and hands me one.

'Cheers.'

We clink cups and take a mouthful.

'Tastes like a fox has fallen in and decomposed,' I say, coughing.

Eden laughs and takes another sip. 'We'll be past caring after a few of these.'

We ease through the bodies into the back garden. Definitely been here before. Spot a kid's trampoline in the corner. Remember Barny using it to try to bounce over the hedge.

'There's Sadie,' says Eden. The party girl, wearing a sparkly silver dress, is surrounded by half a dozen other girls, all dressed to impress. 'Let's go say happy birthday.'

'You go. I've spotted someone.'

'Who?'

'An old friend.'

Barny is leaning against the trampoline, talking to a young woman who clearly got curling tongs for her birthday. My heart goes up through the gears. After my chat with Sharky not sure how he's going to react. Know he prefers Yell's story to mine, but never a better time to put him straight.

I walk tentatively towards him.

'Hi, Barny.'

The cocktail has clearly messed with his vision. He squints at me through eyes that look like paper cuts, before finally dragging me into focus.

'Well, speak of the devil,' he says, with a smile that's ninety per cent snarl. He turns to the young woman and kisses her on the cheek. 'Be back soon, Lexie.'

Barny walks towards the furthest end of the garden. I follow.

When we can walk no more, he turns, his face twisted. 'You've got some cheek coming here.'

'Nice to see you too, Barny.'

'Did Sadie invite you?'

'Not exactly.'

'Still gatecrashing, eh?'

'No, I used the front door.'

'What's wrong with the hedge?' he asks, looking at the wall of green behind him. 'Or have you turned over a new leaf?' He laughs at his stupid joke and takes a big gulp of the toxic liquid.

'Barny, what's all this about? Thought we were mates. Remember when you jumped on that trampoline and tried to clear the hedge.'

He squints at the hedge, then back at me. 'Rather not. It was all crap. We'd got sick of you and your games,' he says, jabbing his finger in my chest. 'Telling us where to go, what to do, as if we were in some kindergarten.'

Know Barny's drunk, but still can't believe what's coming out of his mouth. Thought the guys liked what I did, adding spice to their boring lives. They always laughed at my jokes, went along with my suggestions. Had no idea that peeling back a layer, there was so much hate hiding underneath.

'Nobody made you do it.'

'Your memory's well and truly screwed, mate. You told us we weren't in the gang unless we played your games. They were getting stupider and stupider. You'd become a grade-A loser.'

'If you thought that, why didn't you leave?'

'We were going to. But then...'

'That night... with Yell?'

Barny nods.

I want to hit him.

Put so much into our friendship and this is what I get in return. I move towards him, like a tank, relentlessly forward. He backs into the hedge. Drop my cup on the lawn and grab him by the coat. I'm so close I could get drunk on his breath.

'Do you know what makes me sick to my stomach, Barny? None of you had the guts to say any of this to my face. You've only blurted it out tonight 'cos you've had a bellyful of punch. Any time, you could have said, we've had enough of this, let's stop the games, let's not have a gang leader, let's not have a gang, let's do something else, but no, you were all too chicken. You've dumped me 'cos your parents told you to. You make me want to puke.'

'Hi, guys.'

Eden, smiling as though she's stepped out of a toothpaste commercial.

I let go of Barny's coat.

'Are you going to introduce me?' she says, looking at him.

'No, I'm leaving.'

TWENTY

'COME BACK.'

But my feet aren't listening.

They're taking me further and further from Sadie's house.

'Stop.'

I turn to see Eden struggling to run, hindered by high heels.

My run becomes a jog becomes a stroll becomes a halt. Eden catches up. She grabs me by the arm. 'What's going on?' she pants. 'We'd only been there a few minutes.'

Should have listened to Mum.

Too soon to get involved with anyone.

Way too soon.

'You said if things turned shitty we'd leave. Well, they did. Except it seems I'm the shitty one.'

'What are you talking about?'

'That guy I was speaking to... Barny. Thought he was one of my best friends. Turns out he's joined the enemy.'

'Because of that boy?'

'No, because of me. They've all decided they hate Rory Gordon.'

'What, just like that?'

'No, been coming for some time. The incident with Yell pushed it over the edge.'

'Who's Yell?'

'Eliot Hollings, the guy who's in a wheelchair. Who also happens to be the brother of my ex, Lauren.'

If Eden is shocked, she hides it well.

'Yell told everyone what we got up to. My mates will have been interviewed by the police, the school. Their parents probably put them under house arrest, took their phones off them, stopped their pocket money. And guess who they're blaming?'

'They sound a pretty immature bunch.'

'What does that make me, leader of the immature bunch?'

'I didn't mean it like that. But they can't lay all the blame at your door. They were involved too. Whatever happened to personal responsibility?'

It died.

Eden stares up at the star-speckled sky. 'Ignore him. Move on.'

'Not that easy.'

Time to tell her.

'It didn't end that night on the garden-room roof. Lauren says I'm gonna pay for what happened to her brother. A few weeks back we had a brick through our window with *Rory is dead* written on the side. Someone took our clothes from the line and cut them up. Welcome to my world, Eden.'

She stares at me, open-mouthed. 'Your ex-girlfriend did that?'

'Someone did.'

Eden continues to stare as she absorbs what I've said.

'Lauren dumped me without even listening to my side. She can't see for hating me. I know you're not like that. You should go back to the party.'

'I want you to come.'

'You don't need me in your life, Eden. You should be hanging out with your friends, going to parties, reading *Pride and Prejudice* to Emma or Esther or whatever her name is.'

'I thought I was intriguing,' says Eden.

'You are. But believe me, whatever I am, you don't need. There are plenty of other guys at the party.'

'I don't want them. I want you.'

'Go back to Sadie's.'

'What are you going to do?'

'I'm going home…'

In a dead straight line.

TWENTY-ONE

DON'T CARE ABOUT rules or regulations or cameras or guard dogs or lights or hedges or walls or police. I plough on towards home in a line as straight as I can make. Don't even try to hide my face. If someone picks me up on their camera, so what?

Cheese!

A Labrador sprints from a kitchen and starts running around me, barking loudly. I get down on all fours and bark back as loud as I can, chasing the dog inside, before carrying on. To escape from one garden, find myself on top of a shed. Don't even bother to look at what's on the other side. Leap into space and land in a bush someone's going to have to raise from the dead tomorrow. I cut my hand on a piece of glass embedded in the top of a wall. Suck the blood and continue as if nothing has happened. Get chased by a man with a golf club. Hope his golf is better than his aim. He swings at me four or five times and finds nothing but fresh air.

You need lessons, mate.

No idea how many gardens I get through. Ten, twenty? Maths isn't my best subject. I'll settle for lots. Finally find myself in the road that runs behind ours. Could go around the corner and in by the front door. But that's not what you'd call a straight line. Clear the last fence, up the alleyway and into our garden. Run across the lawn to the back door.

Luckily, it's not locked.

Hear mumbled sounds from the TV.

Go quietly up the stairs.

Not quietly enough.

'Rory, is that you?' shouts Mum.

'No, it's the burglar.'

She's on her own tonight. Dad's out drinking with his brother. Poppy's having a sleepover with a friend. Run to my room. Need to get out of this gear. Mum will have a fit.

Too late.

She is already.

'Rory,' she screams. 'You've left mud all up the stairs.'

My bedroom door bursts open. She stands, staring, as if the ghost of Rory Gordon has appeared.

'What the hell…?'

Catch sight of myself in the bedroom mirror. My best clothes have turned into my worst. They're covered in mud and blood and leaves and dirt. My jacket and trousers are torn, boots scuffed and mud-spattered, my hair all over the shop, my hand dripping blood on to the carpet.

'Did you get into a fight?'

Nearly.

'No, I did Dead Straight Line,' I say, trying to catch my breath.

'What? I thought you were going to a party with that girl.'

'I did.'

But Barny changed all that.

Stare at the blood oozing from my hand.

'This had better be good,' she says, folding her arms.

'No, it's the opposite of good. Barny was at the party. Told me none of them liked being in the gang but didn't have the guts to say so. They hate me.'

'Because of that you decide to come home via people's back gardens?'

'Yeah.'

'Did Eden come with you?'

'No.'

'You left her behind?'

'Yeah.'

'My god, what are you turning into?'

Mum drops into a chair. Her face disappears behind her hands. 'Oh, Rory, Rory, Rory, what are we going to do with you?' Her face reappears, lined, pale, sunken. 'I thought we'd put a stop to all this.'

So did I.

Mum takes a tissue from her sleeve and hands it to me.

'Wipe your hand, Rory.'

Hold the tissue to the cut.

'What about this girl?'

An image of Eden appears in sharp focus. She's standing in the street, asking me to go back to Sadie's with her. Shouldn't have left her there. But then there's plenty of things I shouldn't have done to add to my ever-growing pile of bad decisions. By the end of the year, it'll be a mountain. Maybe Eden's old lady can climb to the top and plant a flag.

'She doesn't need someone like me in her life.'

'Isn't that for her to decide?'

Maybe.

'You gonna tell Dad?'

Hold my breath while she makes up her mind.

'No.'

'Why not?'

'What good will it do?'

Want to hug Mum for saying that. But I'd only get her dressing gown filthy.

'What about our camera?' I say.

Dad's fitted a security system at the back of the house.

'I'll delete the footage.'

Maybe I inherited my sneakiness from Mum.

She gets to her feet. 'I want you to promise me, Rory. You will never, ever, ever play that stupid game again.'

'Sure.'

'Can I have a yes, please?'

'Yes, please.'

Mum shakes her head and heads downstairs.

TWENTY-TWO

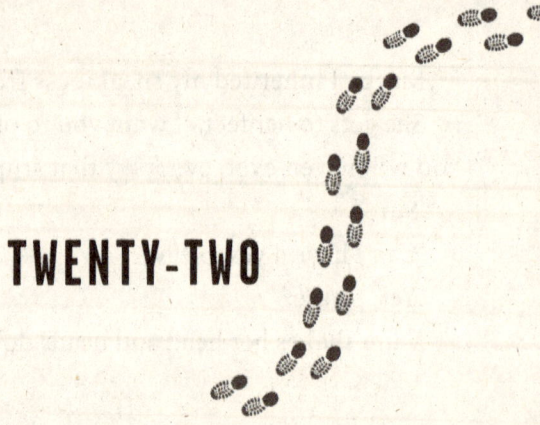

'**CHARLIE, I ASKED** you to be inventive with your writing, but today you've gone too far.'

'What have I done now, Miss?'

She looks down at his paper. 'You said the family sat down to a meal of beef strongenough.'

Laughs escape from behind fingers.

'It's beef stroganoff.'

'Oh.'

I'm back at school. Got there the twisty route: left into Old Park Road, right into Lockerbie Gardens, then on to the bus – which did loads of lefts, rights and roundabouts – then off the bus, left on Mansion Street, right on Dunsford Lane to Hayford Free School. The world's least straight line.

Mum stuck to her word about not telling Dad. Next morning he spotted the bandage on my hand. Told him I cut it on a broken bottle at the party. He was too hungover to probe further. But he did ask how it went with Eden.

We're not going out any more.

That didn't last long.

No, Dad, it didn't.

Saw Eden at school on Monday. She looked through me as if I was a greenhouse.

On Tuesday I said, 'Sorry,' – but that didn't work, and she hurried off to chemistry.

On Wednesday I said, 'Really sorry,' – but the added adverb made no difference and she carried on ignoring me.

On Thursday, I said, 'Can we talk?' – but I was the only one talking, and she escaped into the library.

On Friday, I decided to stop speaking to her. But that didn't mean I stopped thinking about her. Intriguing Eden. I'd only gone out with her for a few minutes, but they were amazing minutes. Walking arm in arm with her up the street, I sensed she got me. Unlike the others. Eden liked me for who I was and didn't care what the haters thought. She thought I was cool. Until the moment I became uncool and ran home like a deer on steroids. There's something about her. And the fact she's ignoring me makes her even more intriguing.

Every now and then, I sneak a look in her direction, but her attention never strays from the teacher.

Do not even think of looking at me, Rory Gordon.

The lesson trundles on through all things English. Grab my bag for fifty minutes of history. We're doing the Cold War, like the one between me and Eden.

'Rory, can I have a word, please.'

Mrs Shields and her famous word. Wonder which she'll choose this time. Idiot, scumbag, miscreant, loser? She's an English teacher, she'll think of something.

I wait for the class to empty and stand in front of her desk, arms crossed, bouncer style. Mrs Shields goes to the door where a couple of girls are loitering, with their listening heads on.

'Out.'

She closes the door and goes back to her desk.

'How's it going, Rory?'

'Life simply keeps getting better and better.'

'Good to hear it.'

My sarcasm seems to be catching.

'What happened to your hand?'

'Tried to karate chop some frozen bread.'

'Do you ever give a sensible answer?'

Not if I can help it.

Mrs Shields shakes her head and opens her laptop. She stares at the screen. 'You haven't been back to Mannings recently.'

'No.'

'Why not?'

'Darwin's got enough points.'

'They're lying third in the house table.'

'Least they're not bottom.'

'Have you given any thought to going back?'

'No.'

'You should. You did a very positive thing, Rory. Giving up your time for others is commendable.'

'The old guy doesn't like me.'

'Not true. The care home's been in touch. Tanker says he'd like you to come back.'

'They understood what he said?'

'Apparently they have someone who's fluent in Geordie,' says Mrs Shields, smiling.

'Why would he want *me*?'

'Why don't you ask him yourself?'

TWENTY-THREE

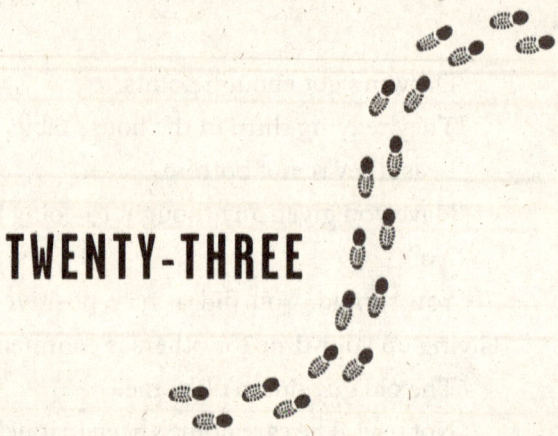

I'M AT THE back of the minibus.

Eden is at the front, as far away from me as possible.

Why am I returning to Mannings? Because I'm bored with pretty much everything. Mum and Dad and Polly and school and brushing my teeth and yawning and Eden not talking to me and studying and Darwin and looking at my phone and not looking at my phone and picking up Biscuit's poo and washing the dishes and going to bed and waking up and going to the toilet and breathing.

Could write a longer list, but I'm too bored.

The only thing I'm not yet bored with is Tanker. But that's only a matter of time. Once he joins the list, I'll quit.

We reach Mannings and troop inside. I get taken to Tanker's room by Hallelujah, a young carer who looks like she's overdosed on happy pills, a big smile fixed to her face.

'Oh, it's so good to see you back, young man,' she beams. 'Makes such a big difference to people like Tanker.'

'Yeah.'

'Imagine you'd rather be out there, playing football with your friends.'

'Yeah.'

'Or with your girlfriend,' she says, with a mischievous look.

Hallelujah is pressing all the wrong buttons.

She knocks on the door of room twenty-two. 'You have a visitor.'

'Enter.'

Hallelujah opens the door. Expect to see Tanker in bed, but he's dressed, sitting in the comfy chair. My eyes are drawn to his trouser leg, cut short, a wrapped stump where his leg should be.

'Y'all reet, Rory, lad?'

'Yeah,' I lie.

'Leave you boys to it. Don't get up to any mischief,' says Hallelujah, and with a booming laugh she exits.

'Sit yersel doon, bonny lad,' says Tanker.

I sit on a plastic chair on the other side of the room.

'Bring yersel closer, man. I'm not contagious.' Shuffle the chair across the floor until I'm within touching distance. 'That's berra. Me eyes aren't what they used to be. Nice to see a young face aboot the place.' He grips the arms of his chair. 'We didn't get off to the best start last time, did we?'

'No.'

'Sorry, I snapped at you 'bout me family, but you touched a nerve. Not your fault.'

'It's okay.'

'Na, it's not okay. You were only tryin'to help. And I fell asleep, didn't I?'

I nod.

'What were you readin'?'

'*Great Tank Battles of the World.*'

'Long as it wasn't the Battle of the Bulge,' he says patting his big stomach. Tanker laughs. It comes with a throaty smoker's cough; the type Grandad used to heave up. 'Na, let's leave the fightin'alone for a bit. Let's talk.'

Rather read. But he's in charge.

'Got any questions for me?'

Yeah, why do two people living on the same island sound like they're from different planets?

'Did you fight in any wars?'

'Just the one. Seventy-two days it lasted.'

'Thought wars went on for ages.'

'Not the Falklands.'

'What's that?'

'Do they not teach it at school?'

'No. The only war we're doing is the Cold War which wasn't even a war.'

'Do you know where the Falklands are?'

Shake my head.

'They're a few lumps of rock in the South Atlantic. You'd think people would find something better to fight over – oil, diamonds, gold. But no, us and the Argentinians fought over a windswept bog covered in sheep crap.'

'Why?'

'Good question. When I was heading sooth on the Canberra, had nee idea. The Argentinians said it was theirs. Thatcher, our Prime Minister, said it was ours. Doesn't take much to start a war.'

'Did we win?'

'We did. But we paid a price. A big one.' Tanker looks outside again. 'Lost some of me best mates.'

'Sorry.'

'Aye, was a long time ago, but remember it like it was yesterday.'

Let the memory do its work, before I speak again.

'Do any of your old army mates visit?'

'Used to meet up. We were that close,' he says, linking his fingers together. 'When you've been through what we did, bonds you tighter than superglue.'

'What happened to them?'

'They're gone. Cancer.' Tanker kicks my foot with his good leg. 'But enough of that. You haven't come here to listen to an old gadgy moan. Tell iz aboot yersel'.'

'Nothing to say.'

'Divvent believe that for a minute.'

He's right. But the last thing Tanker wants is to hear me moan for ninety minutes.

'You look a bit flat, Rory, like you've been run over by a tank. What's the marra?'

Might as well spit it out.

'Split up with a girl.'

'Plenty more fish.'

'This fish was special.'

'You've got years of fishing left, man. But can tell this lass means a lot to you.'

Nod.

'If she's that special, divvent give up on her. I did once. Regretted it ever since.' He takes a sip from a plastic cup next to his bed. 'Hilary was her name. Called her Hil. She was something special. We were together thirty-five year.'

Bang goes another 's'.

'Long time, eh? Wouldn't get that for murder. But that was me – murder. Nightmare to live with. Was in a bad way with me heed. She did all she could to help. I was a right stubborn so and so. Thought I could fix mesel, but was always bad at DIY. Felt I didn't deserve her. Knna it makes nee sense, but that's the way I was.'

Tanker turns away as he struggles to fight off tears.

'Didn't have much in me life, but I had her, and like a silly sod I hoyed it away, like she was a sweetie wrapper.

Too stupid, too arrogant, too stubborn to gan back. Biggest mistake of me life. But I've made me bed, so berra plump the cushions, crash oot and get on with it.'

'Couldn't you get in touch with her?'

'No, lad. We're divorced. Probably found some other gadgy, that doesn't gan radgy.'

I need an English-Geordie dictionary.

'Do you have kids?'

'A son, Nigel. Be in his fifties now. Never hear of him.'

'Why?'

'Wasn't a good father. Back then. I've calmed doon these last few years. Mind yous, had a helluva lot of calming doon to dee.'

A silence descends.

The past is messing with Tanker's present.

Need to do something.

'Would you like me to finish the chapter we were on?'

Tanker shakes his head and grins. 'Na, do yous know what I'd like?'

'What?'

'To gan ootside.'

TWENTY-FOUR

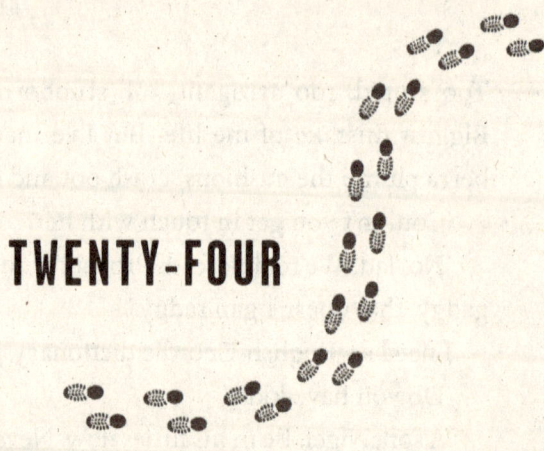

I LOOK AT Tanker, then at the wheelchair.

How am I meant to get him into that? I'm no weight-lifter. He's got to be twenty kilos heavier than me. Tanker reads my mind and pulls on a cord next to his bed.

'Divvent worry, son, help is at hand.'

A moment later Hallelujah appears, grinning as always.

'Room service,' she says.

'I want Rory here to take iz for a push ootside.'

'It's dark.'

'Aye, happens every day.'

'And it's cold.'

'I'm from Newcastle, pet. I'm immune to bad weather.'

Hallelujah looks at me. 'Rory's sixteen. He's only allowed to take you around the gardens.'

'That'll dee. Fresh air is fresh air.'

'Okay, suit yourself.'

Hallelujah folds out the wheelchair, as I help Tanker into his coat. We then get either side of him, a hand under each armpit and, after much grunting and groaning, heave him onboard. Hallelujah takes a thick blanket from his bed and wraps it round him.

'Let's gan,' says Tanker.

I push. Nothing happens.

'There's a brake at the back. Flick it off with your foot.'

Never pushed a wheelchair before. Take the brake off and move the wheelchair slowly out of the room, like I'm a learner driver. Hallelujah accompanies us to the lift. Ease the wheelchair in and we travel down to reception. I'm about to push Tanker out of the front door when Mrs York appears from her office, a look of concern on her face. 'What's going on?'

'Tanker's asked if Rory can take him around the gardens,' says Hallelujah.

Mrs York looks at her watch. 'We don't normally condone night-time walks. As long as you're quick and stay within the grounds.'

'I'm sure Rory will be okay,' says Hallelujah.

'It's not Rory I'm worried about. It's him.'

Tanker laughs. 'Howway, man, let's gan.'

'Enjoy your trip,' says Mrs York.

I push Tanker outside and head towards the garden.

'Not that way,' he says.

'Thought she said to stay in the gardens.'

'They say lots of things here. I wanna gan further afield.'

'How much further?'

'The shops.'

'I was told to stay in the gardens.'

'Not far, man. Second street on the right. I fancy some cheese-and-onion crisps.'

Don't want to disobey Hallelujah or Mrs York, but Tanker's the grown up here, so I push him down the streets, towards his crisps.

Never realised how bad pavements are until I pushed a wheelchair. If it's not cracked paving slabs or steep kerbs, it's great mounds formed by tree roots.

'This is tricky,' I say, trying to manoeuvre over another awkward piece of paving.

'Call this tricky? Imagine driving yersel and the wheel gans over some dog crap.'

'That's happened?'

'Manys the time.'

Note to self. Always take poo bags when I walk Biscuit.

'Cannit beat being ootside, can yous?' says Tanker, letting out a big breath. He starts singing. 'Went to Blaydon Races, 'twas on the ninth of June, eighteen hundred and sixty-two on a summer's afternoon...'

Got a good voice. Croaky, but good.

Tanker said the shops were only two streets away but forgot to ask how long the streets were. Takes us ages to get there. Finally spot them up ahead. Been a while since I was around here, but I recognise the parade. It comprises a kebab shop, an estate agent, a betting shop, a laundrette and a mini supermarket.

Wheel Tanker inside.

'Must be crisps in here somewhere,' he says, looking around the mini-market.

'You've not been here before?'

'Na. Seen the shops from the Mannings minibus. This has been on me bucket list for ages.'

A middle-aged man in a dark-blue uniform approaches us. He speaks to me. 'What are you looking for?'

'Crisps,' goes Tanker.

'They're down the end of the aisle,' says the man, to me. 'Next to confectionery.'

'I'm doon here,' Tanker shouts.

The man walks off, without registering him.

'Always flamin' happens,' Tanker says. 'People talk to the pusher, never the pushed. The price to pay for being waist-high.'

I wheel him down the brightly lit aisle towards the crisps.

Turn a corner.

And crash.

Into another wheelchair.

Yell.

TWENTY-FIVE

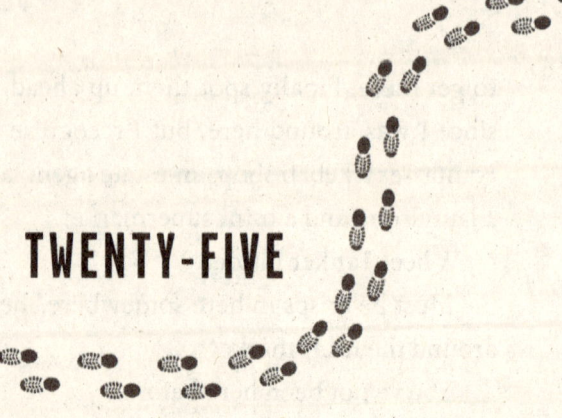

'**GET AWAY FROM** him, Rory,' screams the grey-haired woman standing behind him.

Don't recognise her. But she clearly recognises me. Another one of the Hollings' extra-large family.

Yell stares down at his legs, as if he can't bring himself to look at me.

'I'm sorry,' I mumble, though I'm not sure what I'm sorry about.

'What's gannin on?' says Tanker, confused.

'That lad behind you did this to our Eliot,' screams the woman. 'Put him in a wheelchair.'

'It was an accident.'

'Accident, my foot. *You* pushed him.' She looks down at Tanker. 'Have you injured him as well?'

Need to get out of here. First Lauren, now this. I never want to go to a supermarket again. Spin Tanker around and wheel him along the aisle towards the exit as quickly as I can.

'You should be locked up,' screams the woman. 'You've never owned up to what you did. You're a coward.'

Her ranting fades as I wheel him outside.

'What aboot me crisps?'

I ignore Tanker and push him up the street as fast as the cracks and tree roots allow.

'Rory, stop the bus. What was that all aboot?'

Wait until we're a long way from the shop before I put the brake on and lean against a tree, puffing hard.

'What did you dee to that kid?'

Gobble up some breaths. Didn't want to tell Tanker. Ever. But my secrets keep finding escape tunnels.

'I did something stupid, Tanker.'

He folds his hands across his stomach as he waits for more.

One more breath.

'We used to play a game I made up, called Dead Straight Line. The idea was you had to get home in a straight line, from wherever you were. Meant going through gardens, over fences, hedges. Stupid stuff. But good fun. Until…'

'That lad got hurt.'

Nod.

'He was new to our gang, but not joining in.' Decide not to tell Tanker about Lauren. The story's complicated enough without her barging in. 'I wanted him to prove himself. Got him to do the game one night. Was going okay, until we reached a house with a massive hedge. Only way out was off the roof of their garden room into the neighbours. Yell went first. Didn't know there were concrete blocks below.'

'Come here, lad.'

I move closer and Tanker takes my hand.

'Knew you were carryin' somethin' bad inside you. Could tell you weren't just a shy bairn.'

Tanker lets my hand go. I straighten up and look back at the shops.

'The guy in the wheelchair, Yell, told everyone I pushed him.'

'You didn't?'

"Course not. But nobody believes me.' I look down at Tanker. 'You believe me, don't you?'

He chews on a nail that's got no chew left. 'Haven't seen the facts but seen enough people in me time. Looking at yous, I reckon you didn't dee it.'

Want to hug him. But before I get the chance, I hear voices further down the street.

'What on earth are you doing here?'

Three figures marching towards us.

Hallelujah, Mrs York and Mrs Shields.

TWENTY-SIX

HALLELUJAH PUSHES TANKER back, with Mrs York walking alongside. Imagine they're both fuming. Having given me permission to go into the gardens, I pushed the permission all the way to the shops. I want this evening to be over, but Hallelujah is making incredibly slow progress over the cracks and tree roots. Never walked so slowly in my life. Mrs Shields and I shuffle along some way behind. Don't think she wants Hallelujah or Mrs York to hear what she has to say.

'Rory, you never cease to depress me,' she says, in a loud whisper. 'Just when I think you've got yourself together… you go and do something like this. You were only meant to come and talk to Tanker. You weren't meant to kidnap him.'

'He wanted some crisps.'

'Did Hallelujah or Mrs York say you could go and get crisps? No, they did not. They specifically said you had to stay in the gardens.'

'Tanker wanted them.'

'Oh, so if Tanker said to push him all the way to London, you'd do that?'

'It's only crisps.'

'No, Rory, it's a lot more than that. As a school, we have a duty of care to you and the people at Mannings. These are elderly people. Many of them have serious health issues. They need to stay in an environment where they can be looked after. Imagine if something had happened to Tanker. Would you know what to do? Have you done first aid?'

Stare at my shoes.

'No, I didn't think so. We have to follow their rules and we do not, under any circumstances, break them.'

'Sorry.'

'Me too.'

Never seen anyone look so disappointed in me. Apart from Mum and Dad. And Lauren. And Sharky and Barny. And the woman pushing Yell.

'Why had you stopped on the way back?' she asks.

Mrs Shields walks even more slowly as she waits for my answer.

'In the shop I bumped into Yell, Eliot Hollings, the boy who fell off the roof. Think he was with one of his relatives. She went crazy when she saw me. Screaming all sorts. I pushed Tanker out as fast as I could. He wanted to know what was going on. So I told him.'

'Sorry you had to go through that, Rory, but none of this would have happened if you'd done as you were told and stayed in the care home grounds.'

My fault.

As usual.

If there's a rule needs breaking, call Rory Gordon.

'You going to tell my parents?'

Mrs Shields's tongue works its way around her mouth as she mulls. 'I'll wait and see what action the care home takes. We've spent years building a good relationship with them. This is the first time we've had a major incident.'

Taking an old guy to the shops seems the most minor incident I can think of. But having seen the look on Mrs York's face, they'll probably push for the death penalty.

We finally make it back to Mannings.

'Now go and wait in the minibus till the others have finished,' says Mrs Shields.

'Can I say goodbye to Tanker?'

'No.'

Mrs Shields follows Hallelujah, Mrs York and Tanker inside, while I go over to the minibus. The driver opens the door for me and I climb aboard. While the girls are inside, reading their stories, hoovering up house points, I sit alone at the back of the bus, anger bubbling away. Even when I try to do a good thing, it somehow turns out bad. Why does nothing ever go right for me?

Forty-five minutes later the girls appear. Their chattering stops the second they climb aboard and spot me. Wonder if news of the incident has reached their pierced ears.

The wondering doesn't last long.

'Hear you stole an old person and took him to the shops,' says Rani, a girl from Year Twelve, as she leans over her seat.

'Who told you that?'

'When they couldn't find you in the garden the carers went storming around all the rooms looking for you. They were in a right panic. What did you do that for?'

Because I'm an A-star idiot, Rani.

Eden is the last to climb on board. She looks daggers at me. My body has multiple stab wounds.

'Hope you haven't dropped us all in it,' continues Rani. 'I love Mrs Bradley. And Curie need all the house points they can get.'

TWENTY-SEVEN

THE NEXT WEEK lasts a month.

Expect any moment my parents will call me downstairs to discuss a phone call they've had from the school.

Your son abducted an old man.

But the call never comes. I imagine the care home cops are still thinking what to charge me with. Finally get the message I've been dreading. Mrs Shields wants to meet with me before school starts. My palms are on full moisture-production mode as I make my way, tortoise-like, towards her classroom.

'Rory, close the door.'

Door is shut.

'Sit down.'

Bum is deposited on chair.

'I've heard from Mrs York at the care home.'

A pause. Like one. Of those. Playwrights put in. For dramatic effect.

'She wants to see us both after school. Tonight.'

'Oh.'

'Is there a problem?'

'Yeah, Mum tracks my phone. She'll want to know why I'm going to the care home on the night I'm not meant to be at the care home.'

'Tell her you left a book.'

'What book?'

'You do creative writing. Think of something.'

And so, having told Mum I left my copy of *Animal Farm* at Mannings, I find myself in Mrs Shields's car driving to Mrs York's office, where I'll hear my verdict. Thankfully, Mrs Shields plays music all the way there, so neither of us has to talk about the thing we'd rather not talk about. It's classical music, written before lyrics were invented. Don't care what it is. Anything's better than silence.

Mrs Shields parks her car, and we head across the car park.

'Do your tie up,' she says.

It's droopy, like a windsock without any wind.

I do the knot nice and tight.

'Oh, Rory, look at the state of your shoes,' says Mrs Shields, as her nose creases up like a scrunchy. She pulls a baby wipe from her bag and hands it to me. Shoes are wiped clean, and we head inside.

Mrs Shields takes a breath and knocks on Mrs York's door.

'Come in.'

Mrs York is sitting behind her desk with the sort of expression I imagine she saves for telling families their loved one has passed. Behind her is a colourful sign: *Mannings Care Home. Where Every Day is a Good Day.* Apart from the day I took Tanker to the shops.

'Hello, Flora,' says Mrs Shields, shaking hands with her.

'Hello, Rachel.'

I hold out my hand. Mrs York looks as though she'd rather shake a dead fish. Instead of my hand, she squeezes the end of my fingers, as if they're cows' udders, and quickly pulls away.

'Sit down, please.'

We park ourselves on two plastic chairs in front of her desk. Mrs York leans forward. 'I've called you both here today to discuss the unauthorised removal of Mr Osborne from the Mannings Care Home grounds.'

'Who's Mr Osborne?' I ask.

'Tanker.' She clears her throat and continues. 'It was a most unfortunate incident, and one that we've taken extremely seriously. It's even been to our Board of Trustees.'

'They're volunteers who give advice and stewardship to charities,' says Mrs Shields, assuming I have no idea who Trustees are.

Which is the correct assumption.

Mrs York turns to me with her best death stare. 'Now, Rory, let's consider the facts of this case. Hallelujah and I gave you strict instructions to take Mr Osborne into the care home gardens and nowhere else. Only full-time carers at the home and relatives are allowed to take residents off-site for hospital visits, trips to the dentists and suchlike. We do not allow sixteen-year-old students to take people to the shops for crisps or any other type of sustenance. Do I make myself clear?'

'Yes.'

'Imagine if something had happened.'

Something did happen. I met Yell.

'I'm very sorry,' says Mrs Shields, stealing my line.

'Me too,' I say, in case she thinks my teacher's the only one who's sorry.

'You should never have taken him all that way on a dark, cold night.'

Okay, stop banging on about it.

'But there are mitigating circumstances,' says Mrs York. 'We've spoken at length to Mr Osborne, who says he is wholly responsible for what happened. He said he had a sudden craving for crisps and insisted you took him to the shops. Apparently, you tried to dissuade him, and said it was against care home rules, but he demanded you took him. Is that right, Rory?'

Total fiction.

But let's call it fact.

'Yeah.'

'In light of this, we've decided to take no further action. However, we are instigating a new set of rules. In future only relatives and carers can take any residents out of the building and that includes the gardens. Do I make myself clear?'

'Yes,' Mrs Shields and I say in stereo.

'Thank you for coming over.'

Mrs York rises from her chair and holds out her hand to Mrs Shields.

'Thanks, Flora.'

Mrs York then holds out a hand to me.

'Cheers,' I say.

My hand finally gets a proper shake

'No more nonsense, Rory.'

'No more nonsense, Mrs York.'

Mrs Shields and I exit her office.

'Bullet dodged, Rory.'

'Can I say hi to Tanker?'

Mrs Shields looks at her watch. She clearly has better things to do with her life than spend another evening at Mannings.

'Better clear it with Flora.'

Mrs Shields pops back into the office and appears a moment later. 'Yes, Rory, you can see him, but only for five minutes.'

Hallelujah appears and takes me to the second floor. Her smile is only half its normal size. 'Hope you aren't going to escape out of the window,' she says. 'I got in big trouble over your shopping trip.'

Feel I'm a parrot with a one-word vocabulary. Sorry. Sorry. Sorry.

'I'm sorry, Hallelujah.'

'Apology accepted, but in future Tanker stays in the building.'

'Sure.'

We reach his room.

Knock, knock.

'You have a visitor.'

'Bring 'em in, pet.'

Hallelujah opens the door. Tanker's in bed with a tray of food in front of him. His eyes light up.

'Rory, good to see you, son.'

'I'll leave you two to it,' says Hallelujah, as she closes the door behind her.

I take the comfy seat next to Tanker's bed. 'Thanks for what you said.'

'Little white lie never hurt anyone.' Tanker pushes his tray of food aside. 'Could tell you were in the dung heap when Hallelujah, your teacher and the Camp Commandant turned up. Thought to mesel, why divvent I take the rap. I mean, what's Yorky gonna dee to an old gadgy like me – give me eighty lashes of her tongue?'

'I'm grateful.'

'Aye, can tell you've got enough on your plate. Unlike me,' he says, looking at the tray of food. 'Look at these portions. Not enough to feed a hamster.'

Tanker's right. A solitary sausage, small scoop of potato and a few beans. A guy his size needs more than that.

'Maybe they reckon I need less 'cos I'm missin' a leg.' Tanker shakes his head. 'Portion control they call it. Death by starvation more like it.'

'You never even got your crisps.'

'Nee bother. Doctor says I'm not meant to eat them anyway. And divvent even think aboot smuggling them in. We'll both be for the firing squad.' Tanker picks a crumb from his beard and eats it. 'You still cut up over what that woman in the shop said?'

'Yeah.'

'People will say things aboot yous, but do you knna what, kidda, if you know you didn't dee wrong, that's all that matters.' Tanker takes a plastic cup and drinks some water.

'I'll tell you a story. Got into a fight with a guy in the street once. I was drunk. So was he. Two daft lads tryin' to settle an argument with our fists. Had a go at me for somethin' or other. Probably didn't like the shape of me elbows. Doesn't take much when you're mortal. Took a few swings at me. Wasn't gonna stand for that. Planted one on him. His head hit a lamp-post. Was in a coma for four weeks.'

'Did he die?'

'Not on the outside. But on the inside. His brain was never the same. I got done for grievous bodily harm. The fact I was a solider didn't help. Trained to kill people and all that. Got two year in prison.'

'Even though you didn't mean it?'

'Aye.'

Tanker looks at his reflection in the window. 'Only thing kept me from gannin mad when I was banged up, was I knew I wasn't guilty, or not as guilty as they made iz oot to be. I hit him, but was defendin mesel, that's all. I should have run away, but I was trained never to run. I was a car with nee reverse gear.'

Tanker reaches over, takes my hand and squeezes it.

'Doesn't matter what others think, kidda, there's only one person you've got to believe in… that's yersel.'

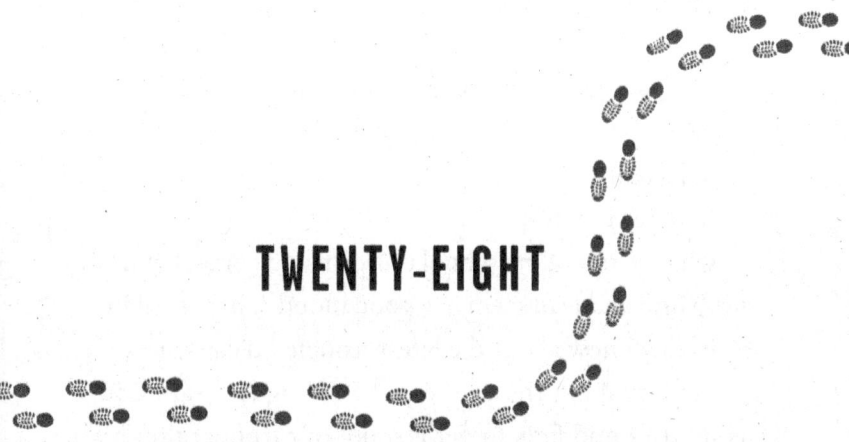

TWENTY-EIGHT

'**RORY, I'D LIKE** you to come back to Mannings,' says Mrs Shields, as she drives me back home.

'Why?'

'We have some serious bridge-building to do.'

Not much of an engineer, but I do owe Mrs Shields a few spans of metal. She stuck by me, when others didn't. Then there's Tanker. He took all the blame for the supermarket incident. Thanks to him I've avoided more punishment. The least I can do is repay him with a few stories about tanks.

'Okay, I'll come back.'

The atmosphere in the car takes a turn for the better. Mrs Shields switches off her classical music, turns on a pop channel and starts singing along to Abba. Nearly ask her if she's ever thought of being a music teacher. But for once my sarcasm remains under wraps.

Mrs Shields drops me home.

'Did you get your book?' shouts Mum.

What book?

'Oh, yeah.'

'Dinner in ten.'

Change out of my school uniform and come down to eat. Mum and Dad seem in a good mood. They wouldn't be if they knew about the latest trouble I'd caused.

'Tell us about this guy you're reading for,' says Dad, as he tries and fails to get a spool of carbonara on his fork.

Don't want to tell them how Tanker fought the Argentinians in the Falklands, left his wife, and went to prison for hitting a guy. Can imagine their reaction.

He is not the sort of role model we want for our son. I'm calling the school.

'He's broad Geordie.'

'Can you have a narrow Geordie?'

'Not sure, Poppy,' I say. 'But I'd never describe Tanker as narrow.'

'What's he like?' asks Mum, nursing a white wine.

'Tanker's been through a lot.'

'Haven't we all,' says Dad, finally getting some strands into his mouth.

He has no idea.

'Why's he called Tanker?' asks Poppy.

'Maybe he's very slow at turning,' says Dad, trying to be funny.

'I don't know, Poppy.'

'Do his family read for him?' asks Mum.

'No.'

'What about his friends?'

'He's on his own.'

'How come no one visits him?' asks Poppy.

'He left his wife, his son. His best friends died.'

Sense a dimmer switch has been turned, darkening the mood at the table.

Might as well carry on turning it.

'He's in a wheelchair.'

There's a moment's silence at my revelation.

'Are you okay about that?' asks Mum, a look of concern on her face.

'Sure.'

'Why can't he walk?' asks Poppy.

'He has diabetes. Got an infection in his left leg. They had to amputate it.'

'Gross.'

'Either that, or he'd have died.'

Bet Dad wishes he'd never mentioned Tanker.

'Are you sure this man is… right for you?'

'What do you mean by that, Mum?'

'Well, after all you've been through. Couldn't they have found someone, I don't know… normal.'

'With two legs?'

'I didn't say that.'

'He is normal, but he's had abnormal things happen to him.'

'I'm sure if it gets too grim, they can find you someone else,' says Dad.

Just because Tanker's not like them and their friends, doesn't mean he's not right for me.

'I don't want anyone else.'

The Tanker conversation comes to a dead stop. The talk disappears down other rabbit holes. Dad talks about a new guy at work who everybody hates. Someone's been in touch with a recruitment company to send him info about new jobs, in the hope he'll leave. Mum talks about her market research company. She's currently recruiting people to explore the future of the underarm deodorant sector. Poppy tells us about a school trip to a museum exploring London's sewage system. I could win a drama award for the way I pretend to be interested.

After we've finished chasing spaghetti around our plates, Poppy and I wash the dishes, while Dad takes up pole position on the sofa to watch a Formula One race he's recorded. Mum puts her coat on. She's off to book club. Their social life seems to be back on track since the police decided not to prosecute me. Guess it's a weight off their minds knowing their son isn't going to prison.

'Have a good night, everyone,' she shouts.

'Bye,' we reply.

I'm trying to remember which drawer the cheese grater goes in when I hear the front door fly open.

'Alan,' screams Mum. 'They've done our car.'

Dad and I race to the hall where Mum stands, white-knuckling the banister.

'Someone's keyed the side,' she says, fighting with her fast breathing to get the words out.

Hurl the tea-towel to the floor and race after Dad. The car is parked a few doors along the street, out of sight of our new doorbell camera. We fire up our phones and turn the lights on the bodywork. It's more than a scratch. Someone has written in large letters on the side.

It was Rory.

'The bastards,' goes Dad.

We look up and down the street, but see no one. Unlike the brick, whoever did this could have keyed the car hours ago. We hurry back into the house. Mum is still in the hall, one hand clinging to Biscuit's collar, the other gripping Poppy, who is on the cliff edge of tears.

'You need to call the police,' says Mum.

'No, I'm going to see the family of that boy.'

'You can't do that, Alan. They've spoken to them already.'

'Fat lot of good that did.'

'You've got no evidence.'

'I don't need evidence. Who else hates Rory enough to have done this?' He turns to me. 'What's Lauren's address?'

'Don't tell him,' shouts Mum.

'What's the address?' he yells, his bulging eyes millimetres from mine.

'Please, Rory,' pleads Mum.

'Forty-eight Melbourne Street.'

Dad races out of the front door.

'What did you have to tell him for?' snaps Mum.

'He'd find out anyway.'

Mum lets go of Poppy and Biscuit and grabs me by the arm. 'You've got to go after him, Rory. You've got to stop him.'

I run outside.

But the car with writing on the side is already disappearing fast up the street.

TWENTY-NINE

RUN TO THE garage and grab my bike.

Haven't ridden it for ages. Feel the tyres with my thumb. They're as soft as week-old party balloons. No time to pump them up. Wheel the bike out of the garage, on to the street and start pedalling like crazy in the direction of Melbourne Street. This is not how I expected to spend my Tuesday night. On a bike chasing my dad in his car, trying to stop him starting a war with Yell's family.

It's further to the house than I remember, especially on two deflated tyres, which send jolts up my bum every time I hit a pothole. There seem to be more holes than road where we live. The closer I get, the more worried I become. What's Dad planning to do? Throw a brick through *their* window, steal *their* clothes, scratch *their* car? Whatever it is, I get the feeling it's going to end badly. Mum's right. He should have called the police. But too late for that. Dad *is* the police. He wants justice.

Finally reach Melbourne Street. I see our car up ahead, badly parked, two tyres on the kerb. Hear the argument before I see it.

'What have you done to us?'

'Get off our property...'

Lean my bike against their hedge and run up the path. Lauren's mum and dad are at the door, shouting. My dad is standing at the bottom of a ramp that leads up to the house. It wasn't there when I last came.

The war suddenly stops. The guns fall silent. Mr and Mrs Hollings both stare at me.

'What the hell you doing here, Rory?' screams Lauren's mum, balling her fists.

'Helping my dad.'

'It's you who's going to need help,' shouts Lauren's dad, picking up a stone garden gnome from the path as he marches towards me.

He doesn't get far. Dad steps in front of him like a nightclub bouncer and grabs his arm, wrestling for the weapon. They are evenly matched. Both unfit and overweight. Neither has the necessary strength to take control of the statue or the situation. Dad gets his foot around Lauren's dad's leg and they topple into a flowerbed.

'Watch my hydrangeas,' screams Lauren's mum.

But when two people think they're right, sense becomes a spectator. The fight continues, the two men causing more damage to the flowers than each other, arms flailing, yet failing to make contact. Curses and grunts fill the air as they continue to destroy the garden. My mind goes back to the story Tanker told me, about the fight outside the pub. A harmless scrap that suddenly turned harmful, when the guy hit his head, causing a lifetime of problems. The same could happen here if one of them gets control of the garden gnome and brings it crashing down on the other's skull.

Need to do something. Take out my phone. I get as far as 99, when I hear a different voice, younger, higher.

'Stop.'

Look up from my phone.

It's Yell. In his wheelchair.

The two wrestlers halt their match as they look back towards the doorway. Dad releases his grip on Lauren's dad who throws the garden gnome away and turns to Yell.

'Go back inside, Eliot.'

'No.'

'This idiot here accused us of attacking his house, his car, stealing their bloody clothes. What would I want clothes like that for?' he says, looking Dad up and down.

'Whatever. Get in the house, Dad,' shouts Yell.

'Yes, Archie,' says his wife. 'You're making a fool of yourself.'

The two dads get up and dust themselves down.

Lauren's dad has the final say. 'I want both of you off my property, or *I* will call the police. I had nothing to do with your crappy car or your clothes, but if you ever come back here again, I promise I will destroy you and your house.'

'Come on, Rory, let's go,' says Dad, realising there's nothing more to be gained from arguing.

We troop back down the path as the front door of the Hollings's house slams shut. Dad and I move slowly up the street towards the car, both trying to find enough breath to form sentences.

'Thanks for coming to my rescue,' pants Dad.

Even though I didn't do much. Apart from make a bad situation worse. I've got a good track record for doing that. I'm so glad Lauren didn't appear. She'd have found something heavier than a garden gnome to hit me with.

'What did Lauren's mum and dad say… before I got there?'

Dad rubs his wrestling arm. 'That they had nothing to do with the attacks. Her dad said if he was going to do something it would be face to face.'

'Do you believe him?'

'He was hardly likely to admit it. I don't know, Rory. I really don't know.'

I lean in and give him a hug. Impressed with Dad tonight. Even though what he did came straight out of the Rory Gordon Playbook of Stupid Things.

He breaks free and runs his hand through his greying hair. 'When's this ever going to end?'

Dad puts my bike in the boot, and we drive off.

THIRTY

BACK AT MY bridge-building class.

Everything's the same at Mannings, except none of the girls from school talk to me, Hallelujah has misplaced her smile and Mrs York looks at me as if I'm about to steal one of her residents. Eden still hasn't forgiven me for running away from the party. Every time I move near her, she goes in the opposite direction, like we're two north pole magnets, repelling each other. That is a bridge that will never be rebuilt.

'Hello, bonny laird,' says Tanker, who's back in his bed, propped against a wall of pillows.

'Hi,' I say, finding a seat and putting my feet up on the edge of his bed.

'Feet off,' he says. '*You* need to be on best behaviour,' he adds, putting every kilo of weight behind the word 'you'.

Take my feet off the bed.

I want to be positive for Tanker, but the attack on the car has removed whatever positivity I had left.

'What's the marra, son? You look like someone's deed.'

'Everything's gone wrong, Tanker.'

'You've got clean clothes, money in your pocket, warm room, food in the fridge, roof over your head.'

'Everyone's got those.'

'I didn't. Lived rough on the street for a long time. You think you've got it hard, Rory, but consider that poor lad in his wheelchair. Imagine what he has to put up with.'

Know he's right. My legs can take me anywhere. Yell is reliant on four wheels to get around, facing obstacles that aren't obstacles to me.

'Feel guilty.'

'And so do I, son, for what happened to that lad in the fight, and all those who didn't make it home from the Falklands. Still gnaws away at me. They call it survivor's guilt, knowing you came through when others didn't.'

'How did you deal with it?'

Tanker looks out at the moonlit sky where some clouds are loitering. 'I had counselling, Rory. Saw things in the Falklands no one should ever see. Carried them aroond with me for years, like bad luck charms. Couldn't get rid of 'em. Couldn't sleep 'cos of 'em. Couldn't function. Took to drink to drown the demons, but me demons were good swimmers, deeing length after length of me heed, like they were trainin' for the Olympics. The demons turned me into one.'

'That when you got help?'

'Na, I was stubborn – a hard man from the Toon, wanted to fix mesel. Except had nee idea how. Then I met another vet, in a similar boat to me, except his wasn't sinkin'. He'd plugged most of the holes. Was gettin' treatment for the things gannin on in his heed.' Tanker takes a sip from his cup. 'Decided to give it a shot. Found I had Post Traumatic Stress Disorder. Except mine was complex. Never dee anythin' straightforward, me.'

'Are you cured?'

'Na, demons still there, but instead of deein lengths, they're deein widths. The counsellin' helped calm me brain doon and get some sleep. Also gave up drink. Took to eatin' instead.' Tanker looks down at where his leg should be. 'Out of the fryin' pan into the fryer.' He reaches over and takes my hand. 'Divvent end up like me, Rory. I blew every chance I had. If something good comes along, grab it and hold on to it and never let it gan.'

'What if bad things keep happening?'

'They'll stop. Just yous wait and see.'

Tanker's turned into a philosopher.

'Tell iz aboot this lass you fancy.'

Tanker's revealed a lot. Time I did the same.

'Eden's from my school. She reads for Emily down the corridor.'

'Plays a canny game of Scrabble, wor Em. Comes up with words that never made it as far as Tyneside. What's gannin on with you and Eden?'

'Invited me to a party. Had a row with a friend and stormed off, left her on her own. Now she won't even talk to me.'

Tanker nods as he thinks.

'When I met wor Hil in Julies in Newcastle, fancied her summit rotten. But the night ended badly. Drunk too many rum and cokes. Was sick on her shoes. Not the best start. But decided I wasn't goin' to give up. Got her home number off a friend and rang her. Said I was dead sorry for what happened. Offered to buy her some new shoes.' Tanker smiles as the memory washes over him. 'Two years later we married.'

Tanker picks up a small, framed photo by the side of his bed.

'Is that her?'

'Aye, us on our weddin' day. Didn't take much when I left, but I took that.'

Tanker and Hilary look insanely happy: him in his smart suit, Hilary in her white wedding dress.

'It's a case of weighin' things up, Rory lad. If the fear of rejection is too heavy, move on, but if the thought of losin' her is heavier still, give it another shot. Divvent live a life of regrets, son.'

THIRTY-ONE

I TAKE OUT my scales.

Fear of rejection. 57 kilos.

Fear of losing Eden. 58 kilos.

Not sure this is what you'd call a scientific experiment. Mr Norman, our chemistry teacher wouldn't approve. *It's not empirical, Rory.* But it proves one thing. I'm not prepared to give up on Eden. Unless, of course, she's even more determined to give up on me.

I plan to sit next to her on the minibus on the way back to school, but she's already sitting next to her friend, Chloe. I can't let this little setback stop me. We get dropped in the school car park. Eden is the first to get out. See her walking quickly towards a car. I leap out and run after her.

'Eden,' I shout.

She carries on walking.

'Eden.'

Get a small grunt for my efforts. She comes to a halt and spins around.

'What you doing?' she snaps.

'Making conversation.'

'Well make something else.'

Not the best start.

'Eden, I'm sorry about what happened. I was bang out of order at Sadie's party.'

'Correct,' she says, folding her arms, like an unamused teacher.

'Can I make it up to you?'

'How?'

'By asking you out.'

'Give me one good reason why I should do that,' she says, her fingers tapping away on her arms as if she's typing her refusal.

Think about what Tanker said, how he'd thrown up on Hilary's shoes and still managed to win her over. I'd only run away from Eden.

'That night at Sadie's party, I was angry with my friend. He said some really shitty things. Messed with my head. Needed to get away. It was super-selfish of me to leave you. You'd done nothing to deserve it. Please don't judge me on one action.'

'What about judging you on two actions.'

'What do you mean?'

'You nearly got us all thrown out of Mannings. Taking that old man all the way to the shops for some crisps. What were you thinking?'

'I was trying to help him.'

'By feeding him ultra-processed food?'

'I'm not a nutritionist.'

'You were told categorically not to leave the grounds.'

Tell me not to do something. I instantly want to do it.

'I felt sorry for Tanker. He wanted some fresh air.'

'Why go all the way to the shops for fresh air? There was some right outside the front door.'

'I made a bad call, Eden.'

'You're the king of bad calls, aren't you?'

Can't argue with that.

'What about giving me a second chance?'

The car toots its horn.

'In a minute,' shouts Eden.

Sense she wants to say something, but not sure what.

'Well?'

The car horn toots again.

'Going to have to go. It's my dad.'

Eden hurries off and climbs into the car.

My chance has just driven away.

THIRTY-TWO

THOUGHTS FLIP TO Yell.

He comes with a lorry-load of emotions. Guilt for taking him out that night. Sadness for what happened to him when he jumped. Anger for the lie he spread. Admiration for getting on with his life. Respect for putting a stop to the Battle of the Dads. I could weigh them and see what comes out on top, but that's too complicated for a science avoider like me. All I know is, Yell has moved into my head and won't be leaving any time soon.

I wonder how he's coping. There are medical advances all the time. Saw a video once of a guy in an exoskeleton. Looked like he was inside a robot, letting him take steps that would otherwise be impossible. Maybe that could be Yell one day.

I count myself lucky.

But my life isn't problem-free.

The police came around after the attack on our car. Said they'd speak to our neighbours to see if anyone had seen anything. Told us they'd notify patrols in the area and gave us a special number to call in case of an incident. They probably have a five hundred horsepower police car for occasions like this. But none of their suggestions actually lead to finding anyone. A couple of cameras caught a figure in black running down the road around the time the car was attacked – none of the pictures were good enough, though, to make out who it was or where they were headed. The identity of the attacker remains a mystery.

There's another problem in our house.

Sleep.

No one can get enough of it. Mum and Dad wander around downstairs at night, preferring shuffling about to the pull of the pillow. Poppy sometimes wakes up sobbing, after another of her nightmares. Even Biscuit seems twitchy, barking at the slightest sound. How do I know this? Because I'm awake too, like a sentry on night duty, waiting for the enemy to attack. Mum used to say I was a member of Gen Zzzzzz, because I slept so much. Not any more.

The worst part is trying to work out what the attacker's plans are. The brick hit the front of the house, the clothes were taken from the back and the car got keyed up the street. Where will they strike next? There are ten eyes and ears in our household (including Biscuit), but it doesn't seem enough.

Neighbours have been kind. Mr Harris put in a security camera too, even though he didn't want one. A lady up the street let us park our car in her garage to avoid another expensive paint job. The mum of one of Poppy's besties, who lives at number twelve, said Poppy can stay over as often as she likes. But, like the police, they're helping with the problem, not solving it.

A piece of good news comes my way, though.

'Hi, Rory.'

'Hi, Eden.'

'I've been thinking about what you said.'

'And?'

'The answer is, drum roll... yes.'

I'd hug her except we're in a class full of students about to start a biology lesson. The next fifty minutes go in a blur. Think Mr Morris talks about anatomy, but he could have been talking about ice-cream cones for all I know. My attention has been stolen by Eden's 'yes'.

The lesson ends. Desperate to talk to her. Follow Eden out of the classroom into a corridor packed with kids. The air is filled with high-pitched voices, all competing with each other to see who can be loudest. Eden ushers me into the library, where we find a quiet spot next to the fantasy section. I back into the bookshelf. Eden gets so close I can smell her mouthwash.

'I will go out with you... on one condition,' she says.

My ears burn with excitement.

'No more running away from me. No more stupid games.'

'That's two conditions.'

'There may be more.'

And this time I hug her, not caring who's looking, or how many more conditions she comes up with.

'Why did you change your mind?' I ask.

'Who said I changed it? I never wanted to hate you, Rory, but what you did made me doubt you. You made me feel such an idiot by running off like that, leaving me alone at Sadie's.'

'I won't do anything stupid again.'

'Hope that's true. For both of us.'

She goes up on tiptoes and kisses me.

*

Normally, I'm in no hurry to get home, but tonight I run all the way from the bus stop, through the front door and hurl my backpack to the floor.

'Training for a marathon?'

'No, Mum, you know the girl who finished with me, Eden?'

'Aha,' she says, looking up from her laptop.

'We've started again.'

'Oh, I'm happy for you, sweetheart. Why the change of heart?'

'She's realised how amazing I am.'

Mum laughs and gets up from the kitchen table to give me a hug.

'Alan,' shouts Mum.

'I'm in the middle of an email,' he shouts back.

'Never mind the email, our son has news.'

Dad trudges downstairs. I tell him about Eden. He's not as happy as Mum, who's watched too many romcoms, but he's pleased in a guy sort of way and fist bumps me. 'Happy for you, Rory. About time we had some good news in this family.'

The doorbell rings.

And rings again.

And again.

And again.

Whoever is there, has a heavy finger.

'Hold your horses,' says Dad, hurrying to the front door, as the bell continues to chime. I follow, keen to know who's so desperate to see us. He opens it to reveal our neighbour, Mr Harris, red-faced and blowing hard.

'Your garden shed. It's on fire.'

Mum has the kitchen blinds down. We have no idea what's going on out there.

Dad and I rush from the hall into the kitchen, followed by Mr Harris.

'What's happening?' says Mum, her eyes prised wide open.

'The garden shed,' shouts Dad.

He reaches the kitchen door and turns the handle. It's like opening an oven that's been on maximum temperature for hours.

'Whooah,' he exclaims.

Arms across our faces, we move tentatively into the garden, getting as close to the fire as the blaze will allow. The entire shed is cloaked in flames. There are sharp cracks, like gunfire, as heat snaps the wood. Flames chew at the branches of the tree above and dense black smoke billows high into the air.

'What the hell,' says Mum, from behind her arm.

'Someone's thrown petrol on it,' goes Dad.

'I'll get the hosepipe,' shouts Mum, looking at the long snake of plastic at the back of the house.

'No, we need to get inside,' says Dad.

'Why?'

'Just get inside.'

But it's too late.

The garden shed explodes.

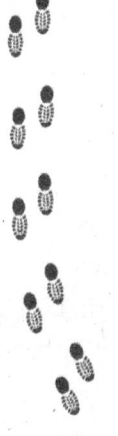

THIRTY-THREE

TANKER STARES AT me as he takes in the aftermath of the arson attack. The bandage on my head, the plasters on my face, the cuts on my hands.

'Someone's been in the wars,' he says. 'What happened, son?'

'Our attacker came back. Set alight the garden shed.'

'That how you got your injuries?'

'Yeah, but it wasn't the shed, it was what was inside. A petrol mower, full of fuel. The flames ignited it. The shed went off like a bomb, sending burning wood flying in every direction.'

'Anyone else hurt?'

'Mr Harris, our next-door neighbour, my mum, my dad. Just as well Poppy wasn't there. Dad was closest and got the worst of it. Was hit by a big piece of wood. Needed a ton of stitches and painkillers for the burns.'

Tanker shakes his head in disbelief.

'Mum called the emergency services. Never seen so many vehicles. Fire engines, ambulances, police cars.'

'Fires are deadly, man. Could have killed someone.'

'That's what the police said. Had their forensics people on the scene, looking for clues. If they didn't take it seriously before, they do now.'

'I'm sorry, lad. What you gonna dee?'

'Mum wants us to move house. But if we stay in town, it won't be hard to track us down, and if we move to a different part of the country, who's to say they won't follow us.'

'Aye, you cannit run from your enemy. Only makes 'em stronger. You've gotta take the battle to them.'

'What's the worst you've been in?'

Tanker looks down at hands that scrunch his blanket tight. Takes time before his lips start moving again.

'Never told anyone this before. Always kept it buried.'

'You don't have to tell me.'

'You could be the last one to hear it. Might as well spill the beans.'

Tanker folds his hands together, briefly closes his eyes and begins. 'It was the battle for Mount Longdon, the Falkland Islands. June 1982. I was in 3 PARA, B Company. We set off in rain that cold, was like being stabbed in the face with icicles. Awful it was. Winter in the South Atlantic, not the place to gan for your holidays. Didn't even have proper boots. But what we did have was determination. To get the job done.

'We were headin' towards the capital of the Falklands, Port Stanley, which was held by the Argentinians. In the way was Mount Longdon and two other mountains, Harriet and Two Sisters. Friendly soundin' places, eh? Didn't end up friendly.

'We tabbed toward Mount Longdon. Had three objectives called Fly Half, Wing Forward and Full Back. Some rugby mad officer must have come up with that. The Argentinians were expecting us from the north, so we approached from the west, even though we knew they'd planted landmines. We fixed bayonets and set off just after midnight. Wanted the element of surprise, but wor plans were blown up, literally. A corporal stood on a landmine. His screams alerted them, and that was that. Let battle commence as they say. All hell let loose.

'It was old-fashioned warfare, Rory. Grenades, gunfire, bayonets – the lot. Some of the lads were only a bit older than ye, seventeen or eighteen, but they fought like tigers. It was carnage. Someone must have been watching over me, 'cos I came through it in one piece. Others weren't so lucky. Guys lost arms, legs, stomachs blown open by shells and shrapnel. It wasn't just us. We came across Argentinians, dead and dying, some of them screamin' for their madres.

'Even when we took Mount Longdon later that mornin, it wasn't over. We stayed under heavy artillery fire for another day and a half.' Tanker swallows a gulp. 'We lost twenty-three men on that mountain.'

Can't imagine what it must have been like. I only had to jump over a few fences and hedges. He had bullets and missiles fired at him by people out to kill him. And some of the soldiers, only seventeen, a few months older than me.

'I'm sorry.'

'Wasn't your fault. General Galtieri started it.'

I'll Google him later.

'Was it always like that in the army?'

'Na, most of the time was dead borin', waitin' for somethin', anythin', to happen. Remember in Northern Ireland we stayed on rooftops for hours with binoculars lookin' for trouble. Some of the guys hid in hedges for days waitin' for people they thought were up to nee good.'

Tanker looks outside as rain batters his window.

'Wish I could call up some of me old marras in 3 PARA. They'd sort it oot for yous.'

He doesn't need to do that.

I can sort this myself.

Tanker's given me an idea.

THIRTY-FOUR

'EDEN, I HAVE a favour to ask.'

'What?' she frowns.

'For the next few weeks, when you go to Mannings, can you take my phone with you.'

'Why not bring it yourself?'

'I'm not going. Need to study for my mocks. Mum says I'm way off my predicted grades.'

'This is making no sense, Rory. You want *me* to take *your* phone to Mannings because *you're* studying.'

'It's too much of a distraction.'

'Why not switch it off. Put it in a drawer.'

'I'll find it.'

Eden studies me as though I'm a surrealist painting. One she's struggling to make sense of. 'This has got nothing to do with studying for your mocks, has it? What are you up to, Rory Gordon?'

'Can't tell you.'

'Then I won't take your phone,' she says, folding her arms defiantly.

I need her to do this, or the house of cards I'm building will come tumbling down. Mum mustn't find out where I am. Pretty sure she spends more time watching me than she does property programmes.

'Okay, but if I explain, you've gotta promise not to tell anyone, especially my mum and dad.'

'I've never even met your mum and dad.'

'But you might. Some day.'

After what happened with Lauren, I'm nervous about taking Eden home to meet my parents. And after what happened with Yell, guess Eden is nervous about me meeting hers. She never talks about them.

She mulls for a moment.

'Okay, I promise.'

Eden is the only one I can trust to keep this secret.

I tell her my plan.

After I've finished Eden stares at me, as though I've grown an extra head. 'Rory, this is insane,' she says, her voice rising. 'Thought you were going to stop your stupid games. You promised me.'

'It's not a game. It's a plan that might work. I have to do this.'

The scratches on our car was Dad's breaking point. The exploding garden shed was mine. I've had enough. And so have Mum and Dad. Their scars are healing, the bruises fading, but I can tell they're traumatised by everything that's happened. Who knows what the splinters of wood have done to their minds? Look at Tanker, still battling his demons, years after the fighting stopped.

Eden touches my cheek tenderly. 'What if it goes wrong?'

'Leave the worrying to me. You have to help me, Eden. Imagine this happening to your family – what would you do?'

'Not this. You've no idea it's going to work.'

'But if I do nothing, it *definitely* won't work. I can't sit around on my bum all day staring into space. You've no idea what this has done to my family. You have to do this, Eden. Please take my phone?'

She considers it for what seems like an eternity.

Then finally, the word I've been waiting for.

'Okay.'

THIRTY-FIVE

TELL MRS SHIELDS I won't be coming to Mannings for a few weeks. She's disappointed, but the disappointment melts away like one of Mrs Harding's glaciers when I tell her why. Need to put in some extra studying for my mocks, as I'm behind with my predicted grades. Mrs Shields swallows it whole, pleased I'm knuckling down, but sad I won't be seeing Tanker for a while.

And so, for the third Thursday in a row, instead of my nose buried in a book, my body is buried in a hedge in the front garden of Mr and Mrs Hadley, our elderly neighbours who live opposite us on Yatesbury Avenue. For a couple of hours a week, from my uncomfortable position among the leaves and branches, I look for anything strange going on in our street. Could have chosen the back of our house, but after what happened with the garden shed reckon whoever is attacking us won't go that way for a while.

Tanker loved my idea. Even gave me some tips.

Wear the warmest clothes you can find – thermals if you've got them. Consider everyone a suspect, never let your attention stray and make sure you go to the toilet before you start.

The surveillance operation is planned with military precision. I take a backpack to Hayford Free with a change of clothes and trainers. When school finishes, I give my phone to Eden, go to the toilet, do any business that needs doing, change out of my uniform into outdoor gear, put my school stuff into my backpack and make my way to our street. When no one's around, I crawl inside the Hadley's hedge.

Trips to Mannings last about two hours, so that's how long I spend in the foliage. When Eden's finished, she drops my phone in the mailbox in front of our house. Once I see Eden and her dad drive off, the surveillance is officially over. No idea what she tells her dad, but Eden's smart. Sure she comes up with something credible. I then crawl out of the hideaway, pocket my phone and go home. If Mum or Dad ask why I'm wearing outdoor gear I'll tell them I'm helping decorate Tanker's room.

I could never be a spy. Watching our street is the most boring thing two eyeballs can do. Man walks dog. Two teenagers go past on scooters. Old couple walk slowly down road, arm in arm. That's the first ten minutes. If they ever make a programme called *Rory's Street*, whatever you do, don't watch it. You will die of boredom. On top of that, the hedge is cold and unbelievably uncomfortable.

I should have got sponsored.

Rory's Hedge Challenge. Sponsor him for every minute he stays stuck in twigs.

One time a dog stuck his nose into the bush, sniffing about. For a horrible moment thought he was going to pee on me. Thank goodness, the owner pulled his lead and took him away.

Check my watch.

6.47 p.m.

Only forty-three minutes until Eden comes back with my phone, and I can go home, have a warm bath and defrost. Then I see him. Someone in a dark hoody walking quickly along the street, head down, carrying something in his hands. He looks around, furtively, then stops right in front of my hiding place. He's so close could almost touch his legs. He's holding small bags. Walks up and down as though he's looking for something. Worried he's going to find me, but he stops pacing, pulls on a mask and hurries across the road towards our house.

Fear squeezes my stomach tight. But curiosity overpowers my panic. Need to know who it is. I extricate myself from the hedge as quickly as four stiff limbs will allow and run after him.

'Oi,' I shout.

Whoever it is, throws the bags into our front garden and sprints away.

'Stop,' I yell.

He carries on as fast as he can. I race after him. Not as fit as I was when I hung out with the gang, but a combination of anger and revenge makes up for lack of training. Find a gear I never knew my engine had.

This guy is fast.

But I'm not giving up.

Our street leads on to Mason Avenue then Hardwick Road, which has lots of shops and bars. There'll be people out at this time of night. I'll shout for help. Hopefully, someone will be up for a bit of rugby tackling, or happy to stick out a foot. He doesn't head into Hardwick Road, though. Whoever is behind the mask takes a sharp left into a driveway and up the side of the building.

Promised Mum I'd take no more short cuts.

Promised myself I'd catch whoever's doing this.

My promise wins.

I race up the driveway after him. He jumps on to a recycling bin and clambers over a wooden fence into a back garden. I follow and land on a gravel path in an alleyway at the side of a house. Security lights come on and I spot him, twenty metres ahead, running across the lawn. The garden seems to have no exit points, but there's a low bank of bushes, separating it from its neighbour. Without hesitating, he dives forward and is swallowed by the wall of green, like some suburban stuntman. I take a deep breath and dive after him. The bushes hurt like hell, adding to the cuts on my face and hands, but the painkiller known as adrenalin goes to work. Land heavily on a lawn and clamber to my feet. He's sprinting down the side of the house.

The warm clothes I'm wearing are perfect for hiding in a hedge. Not so good for an evening run. Every pore is working overtime on sweat production. But I can't stop now. Might be my only chance to catch him. Pound up the gravel path at the side of the house, into the front garden and on to the street behind it. Again, he proves he's a path-dodger and heads for the house opposite. It has large metal gates. He finds a foothold and starts to scramble over. Grab his trainer, but he kicks me in the head with his other foot. I topple back. Before I can get to my feet, he's over the top, tearing towards a wooden security door blocking the way. He vaults over. Gasping for breath, I follow.

Into another back garden.

But we're not alone.

A black Alsatian appears from the darkness, barking with all the noise a four-legged burglar alarm can. The dog runs around the guy, snapping at him, but he doesn't stop and clears another fence. The dog turns its attention to me. It's all the incentive I need to defy the laws of gravity and soar over the fence. Land heavily. I don't want to do this any more. My lungs feel they've quadrupled in size, my machine-gun breathing unable to fill them. My muscles are worn out and need replacing. My blood has been replaced by lactic acid, burning my legs, begging me to stop. But rest is for tomorrow. I have to keep going.

Look up, gasping. The guy changes direction. Instead of heading up the side of the house, he runs over to a garden room that overlooks the neighours. He's planning to jump from there into the garden next door. The room is smaller than the one Yell jumped from, but still a major obstacle. He grabs a chair from beneath a table and moves it to the side of the building. I'm almost on him. Instead of using the chair to climb on to the roof, he hurls it at me. I throw myself to the ground, and the chair sails harmlessly over my head.

Now he's trying to haul himself on to the roof with his arms. But he's not strong enough. I grab hold of his legs and yank him down. He falls on his back on the lawn. I jump on top of him as he wriggles beneath me and rip off his balaclava.

Can't believe who's staring back at me

It's Sharky.

THIRTY-SIX

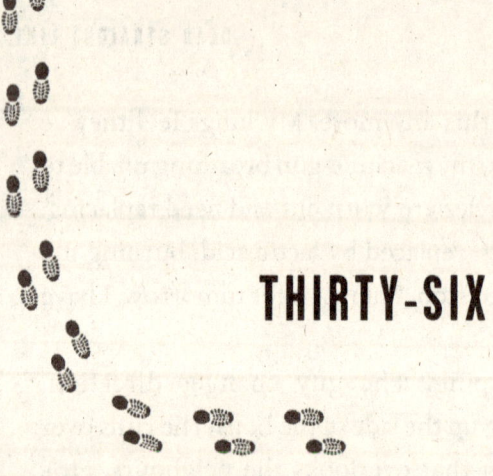

SHARKY TRIES TO wrestle free.

I punch him hard in the face.

The squirming stops.

'Why the hell did you attack our home?' I scream.

Have no evidence Sharky is responsible, but how many people run through strangers' gardens at a hundred miles per hour to evade capture unless they've done something wrong? He doesn't seem keen to talk. I raise my fist again.

'Lauren,' he mutters, through bloodied teeth.

'What's she got to do with it?'

'Lauren's my girlfriend.'

Lower my fist and the lightbulb goes on. All becomes clear. Sharky goes out with Lauren. She gets him to do her dirty work. Win-win for them. Lose-lose for us.

'She put you up to this, didn't she?'

Can tell Sharky doesn't want to say more, but nor does he want to spend tomorrow at the dentist. He knows I'm stronger than him and won't stop until I have the answers I'm looking for. He turns and spits blood on to the grass. Then he turns back to me.

'She said if I wanted to keep seeing her, I needed to show some loyalty.'

'What about your loyalty to us?'

Thought that's what our gang was all about. Supporting each other. Seems Sharky decided to support someone else, like a kid who switches football teams because theirs isn't winning.

'You threw a brick through our window.'

'I wanted to stop after that, seriously, but Lauren kept on at me to keep going. "I want bigger and better spectaculars," she said. "I want Rory and his family to suffer, the way we have."'

'But what have we ever done to you?'

His reply is slow in coming.

'Nothing.'

'So why did you do it?'

'I wanted to make her happy.'

'By setting alight to our garden shed, by injuring Mum, Dad, me, our neighbour?'

'I didn't want to hurt anyone. How was I to know it would explode?'

'Ever heard of petrol mowers?'

'Didn't think.'

'Thinking's never been your strong point.'

Lauren, Lauren, Lauren. Ever since that party, Sharky had the hots for her. Always seemed jealous when he saw us together. Can imagine the excitement on his face when he asked her out and she said yes. If that's how it played.

'Did you ask her out?'

Sharky shakes his head. 'No, she came on strong to me.'

Why on earth would she go out with a loser like him? Because he was the perfect person to do her dirty work. That way she and her family would be in the clear. Should have known one of the gang was responsible. Who else escapes that easily across back gardens? Knows how to climb over fences, clamber through hedges, quietly and quickly? No wonder he was so scared the night I sneaked from my bedroom to meet him. He'd already lobbed a brick through our front window and was planning more attacks to please his girlfriend. He couldn't wait to get to the safety of his house.

'You disgust me, Sharky. I thought we were mates.'

Want to hit him again, but much as he deserves more pain, my hands don't. I've wasted enough energy on him tonight. I roll Sharky on to his front, take off my belt, and tie his hands behind his back.

'What you doing?' he mutters.

Wait and see.

I drag him to his feet.

'Where you taking me?' he says, his voice cracking.

'My house.'

'No, Rory, don't, please. I'll make it up to you.'

'How do you plan to do that? Put our window back in, buy us new clothes, respray our car, build us a new shed? You are gonna pay for this, Sharky, in ways you never imagined.'

'Mum'll kill me.'

'Not unless my mum kills you first.'

I lead him across the garden towards the house. A kitchen light goes on and a middle-aged woman in a onesie appears at the back door. 'What the hell are you two doing in my garden?'

'Looking for our football.'

'I'm calling the police.'

'Well, if you do, send them around to 25 Yatesbury Avenue.'

She stares at us, open-mouthed, as I push the blood-spattered Sharky up the passage at the side of her house and on to the street. He pleads with me all the way back not to hand him over, but I didn't spend all those hours in a hedge to go home empty-handed. I reach our house, open the gate and push him up the path. See half a dozen green poo bags on the grass. That was going to be his next stunt.

I open the front door and push him inside. Mum and Dad appear in the hall, still wearing the battle scars from the explosion. Hard to tell which of them looks most shocked.

'What the...?' says Dad, putting the brakes on his expletive.

Mum looks down at her phone. 'Rory, what are you doing here? According to this you're on the way back from the care home.'

'I'll explain later.'

'Why have you brought Sharky here... tied up?' says Dad, looking at the belt around Sharky's hands.

'And why is he bleeding?' asks Mum, as blood continues to ooze from his lips.

'Because he has something to tell you... don't you, Sharky?'

THIRTY-SEVEN

SHARKY TRIES TO shovel the blame on to Lauren.

I shovel it back on to him.

'It wasn't as if she had a gun to your head, Sharky. You could have said no any time. Because she asks you to do something doesn't mean you have to do it.'

The same argument I used with Yell and Dead Straight Line.

The argument that failed to save me.

'I'm disgusted with you, Finn,' says Mum, her arms folded tight across her chest. 'How could you do this to us? What have we ever done to you?'

Sharky has no answers. He did it because Lauren would dump him if he didn't. He was mad for her. He was in her thrall. Simple as that.

'How come I never heard anything about you and Lauren?'

'We kept it a secret.'

Figures. Lauren's mum and dad would go ballistic if they found out she was seeing another member of the gang. Sharky's mum would be far from happy if she found out he was dating my ex. And if I'd discovered they were going out, wouldn't need to be Sherlock Holmes to work out who was behind the attacks.

'Met in quiet places, went to films no one else would watch. That sort of thing.'

'Bet that was her idea as well.'

He nods.

'So how long were you going to keep on attacking us?' says Mum, her face flushed with anger.

'I wanted to stop, but Lauren kept saying one more… one more.'

Mum and Dad shake their heads in disbelief.

'To think we had you round for dinner here,' says Dad. 'You played football in our back garden. We went to the beach with you.' He then turns to me. 'Rory, I can't believe you'd hang out with someone like this.'

Trust Dad to try to involve me in the attack on my own house.

'Can I call my mum?' mumbles Sharky, through two swollen lips.

'You'll need to call your solicitor. I'm ringing the police.'

Unless the woman in the onesie has called them first.

'No, Alan. Let him speak to his mum.'

'You've got to be kidding. After what he's done.'

Dad gets his phone out and calls the emergency services.

Can't bear being in the same room as Sharky a second longer.

'Take this,' I say, offering Dad the belt that tethers Sharky's shaking hands. He takes the belt and I go into the sitting room. My brain is back in the blender again. Look at our new coffee table. Can't believe one of my best friends smashed the old one. I pace the carpet that we vacuumed for ages, searching for glass. How could someone who was so close to me, become so evil? I'm only on pace number ten when a car pulls up outside our house. Police must have broken the speed limit to get here that quickly. Pull back the blinds. It's not the police. It's Eden. Dash past Mum, Dad and Sharky to see her putting my phone in our mailbox.

I run up to her. She looks up, stunned.

'Rory, what are you doing home?'

'I caught him.'

Her face breaks into a nervous smile. 'How?' she asks.

'How do you think? I jumped out of the hedge and ran after him.'

'Wow... that's great,' she says, although her 'wow' lacks the wow factor. Guess the news means a lot more to me than it does to her.

'It was... Sharky.' His name feels like sick in my mouth. 'One of our gang.'

'Sharky, your friend? Why would he do that?'

Struggle to tell her the story. It's like scratching an itch. One that's only going to bleed.

'He's going out with Lauren, Yell's sister. She was egging him on.'

'That's... terrible.'

Toot from her dad's car horn.

'There in a minute,' she shouts.

Eden seems on edge.

'Is everything okay?'

She looks at the pavement.

'Something's happened. It's Tanker. He's been taken to hospital.'

THIRTY-EIGHT

NEXT DAY AFTER school, Eden and I catch the bus to St James's hospital to see Tanker. Tell her everything Sharky told me last night. Reckon she'll have a ton of questions for me. Instead she looks out of the window, lost in her thoughts.

'Never seen you so quiet.'

'Lot to take in, Rory.' She squeezes my hand. 'Can't believe his obsession with Lauren would make him do things like that.'

'Guys can do crazy stuff.'

'So can girls.'

Should feel good about last night. Instead, it makes me want to vomit. Feel utterly betrayed by my ex-girlfriend and ex-friend. Capturing Sharky is a victory that seems more like a defeat.

We get off the bus and walk hand in hand through town.

'Did you say anything to your mum and dad about what happened?' I ask.

'No. None of their business.'

'What did you tell your dad you were dropping off in our mailbox?'

'Said you were studying for your mocks and that the guy you read for, Tanker, liked to send you notes from his diary. Show you what he's been up to.'

Never knew Eden was such a good liar.

We approach the hospital.

'Hate these places,' I mumble.

'Why?'

'People go in alive. And come out dead.'

'Not everyone.'

'But enough.'

'You've got to stay positive, Rory.'

Google put a stop to that. Mrs Shields told me Tanker has pneumonia. Went online and read about it. It was a biology lesson I'd rather not have had. Thought pneumonia was like a cold, but it's a lot worse than that. Can lead to a wheelbarrow load of bad things – sepsis, shock, respiratory complications, heart problems. It kills over forty thousand people every year. Tanker avoided bullets and shells in the Falklands but got cut down by a chest infection.

'I feel guilty. Haven't seen him for weeks. While I've been hiding in a bush, Tanker's been getting sick.'

'It's not your fault, Rory.'

Haven't heard that expression.

For about a million years.

We walk through the sliding doors into the highly polished hospital entrance. See lots of people sitting in chairs, waiting for the news that will make or break them. Mum told me patients in hospital are only allowed two visitors at a time. I told her not to worry. Tanker doesn't know anyone.

'We're here to see Mr Dave Osborne,' I say to the receptionist. 'He was admitted yesterday.'

She checks her laptop. 'He's in Ward 2M, on the second floor. Lifts are over there.'

We take the lift to the second floor, wash our hands with gel, put our face masks on and enter the ward. There are half a dozen beds in here. Tanker is in the corner. Looks as if he's aged ten years since I last saw him. He seems to have shrunk in size.

'Here come the bank robbers,' says Tanker, as we come into focus.

'Hi, Tanker.'

'Hi, Rory.'

'This is Eden.'

'Alreet pet,' he says, with laboured breath, as though each word is being dug out with a shovel. 'Why've you been keepin' her from me?'

'She reads for Emily.'

'Lucky old Em. And I get the short straw,' he says, his eyes lighting up as he grins. 'Only joking, Rory, lad. You've been an absolute star.'

'We brought you some fruit,' says Eden, putting a bag on his bedside table. 'Hospital won't let us bring flowers.'

'Aye, fruit's berra; flowers taste flamin' awful.'

Eden and I sit on plastic chairs at the side of his bed.

'They told me what happened,' I say.

'Aye, pneumonia. Should be gettin' old monia at my age.'

'Not damaged your sense of humour.'

'That'll be the last thing to go. Once that's gone, I'm toast.' Tanker looks at me, then Eden. 'What news?'

Eden looks outside, as if she can't bear to hear the story again.

'I caught the guy who's been attacking our home.'

Tanker claps his scrawny hands. 'That's marvellous, man. The surveillance worked?'

'Like a dream. Hid in a hedge, like you said. Thought he was never gonna show up, but he did. Long story short, I ran after him and caught him.'

'Hope you beat seven bells out of him. Not that I condone violence, like. Apart from when people ask for it. And if they ask for it, you've gorra give it to them. Be rude not to.'

'I gave him what for.'

'Good, lad. Who was the gadgy?'

'A friend... who'd turned into an enemy. That's what hurts the most.'

'There's nothing worse than someone you thought you could trust, turning against you. Had a dog like that once. Sweet as anythin'. Until the day he decided to take a chunk oot of me.'

'How are you feeling, Tanker?' asks Eden, changing the subject.

'Fair to piddlin', pet. This has knocked iz for six. I'm knackered all the time. At night if it's not the gadgies in here coughin' their guts oot, it's nurses giving me a tablet at stupid o'clock. Spend all day dreamin' aboot sleepin'.'

Eden smiles.

'Would you like me to get in touch with anyone?' I ask.

Tanker goes quiet, his hand scrunching the sheets.

'Na. Happy for you twos to visit.'

'What about Hilary and your son?'

'Caused them enough grief. Divvent want to add to it.'

'They might be worried…'

'Na means na, alreet?'

'Alreet,' I reply. 'But if you change your mind.'

'Me mind's not like underpants. Doesn't need changing.'

Can't push this any more. Tanker's an immovable object.

'Would you like us to read to you?' asks Eden, sensing the mood has taken a wrong turn.

'Belter. What you got?'

I pull a book from my jacket. '*All Quiet on the Western Front.*'

'Oh, that'll cheer iz up no end.'

'We could get something else from the hospital library,' says Eden.

'Na, that'll dee, pet. The Germans suffered every bit as much as wor lads. People need to know that.'

'Thought we could alternate. I'll read first, then Eden.'

'What more could a couple of hairy ears want?'

We start Erich Maria Remarque's harrowing story as Tanker listens. Eden reaches the end of the first chapter. *'Young men of iron. Young? None of us is more than twenty. But young? Young men? That was a long time ago. We are old now.'*

She glances up. Tanker's snoring. He's finally found the sleep he was looking for.

'What should we do?' asks Eden.

'Leave him. He needs sleep more than he needs another battle.'

Eden moves the blanket over his hands and tucks it around him.

'Bye, Tanker.'

I touch his hand, and we leave.

THIRTY-NINE

SHARKY'S IN TROUBLE.

He's in so deep, sunk to the very bottom of an ink-black pool. After I told the police what happened he was taken off to the station. They turned a blind eye to the fact I'd been hiding in someone's hedge, careering through gardens I shouldn't have been in and that I'd punched him. They know what my family has been through. Found out later Sharky admitted to everything and was charged with arson, theft and criminal damage to endanger life.

His mum, Ellie, rang Mum to apologise. She didn't get past 'sorry' before Mum cut her short. Said she was too upset to talk right now. Guess some day they'll sit down over a coffee, united by their common problem: a son who betrayed their trust.

Sharky wasn't the only one swimming in sewage.

Lauren was caught in it too.

Heard on the grapevine the police had interviewed her. She denied everything, of course. But the police had Sharky's confession and phone records detailing conversations he and Lauren had had about the attacks. Her phone also showed she was close to our house at the time of the attack on our garden shed. Even Lauren's tongue wasn't nimble enough to worm her way out of that. She too has a punishment heading her way. Not sure she and Sharky will be getting engaged any time soon.

When I think about Lauren and the lengths she went to to hurt me, makes me even happier I found Eden. A girl overflowing with hatred replaced by one who was prepared to forgive me for everything I'd done.

For the first time in a long time, my life is calm. But a flat sea is only temporary. I'm studying at my laptop when I get an email from someone I never expected to hear from again. My old headteacher.

Hello Rory,

Hope you are well.

I've heard the awful news about Finn Edwards. He is no longer at Copsem High and I'm sure will be dealt with by the authorities in an appropriate manner.

I'm writing to ask if you would kindly come into the school at a time that is convenient to you. I have something I wish to discuss.

Best wishes,

Richard Thomas

Headteacher, Copsem High School
Currently reading: *War and Peace*

Close the laptop.

Why would Mr Thomas want me to go back to Copsem? He's excluded me once. He can't do it again. Must be something super-important for him to write to me. I ask Mum what she thinks about his email. She has no idea but says there's only one way to find out.

Hate the guy.

But also curious.

Curiosity wins. After extra time.

Arrange to meet him at 6.30 p.m. next evening, when there are no pupils about. I catch the bus to Copsem and walk across the playground. Seems weird being back – a place where I caused so much mayhem, now spookily quiet.

Stroll the squeaky corridors to his door.

Knock. Knock.

'Come in.'

He's at his desk typing. Probably writing to some parents to tell them their child is not the angel they think they are and is about to be banished to hell.

'Take a seat, Rory.'

He stops typing and leans over his desk to give my hand a good shake. 'Thanks for coming in. How's it going?' he says cheerily.

'Okay.'

'So sorry to hear about everything your family has had to deal with. Can't believe Finn was involved. He seemed such a... quiet lad.'

If he's brought me here to talk about Sharky I'm on the next bus home.

Luckily, the conversation chooses a different path.

'What's Hayford Free like?'

'A big building with loads of classrooms and corridors.'

Mr Thomas laughs. 'Same old Rory.'

'What's this about?'

Mr Thomas flicks the switch all teachers have. The one that turns them from trivial to serious in a heartbeat.

'We've been having some trouble at school.'

'Not my fault.'

'I'm not saying it is. Nevertheless, you are to blame... indirectly.'

Clench my fists underneath his desk. 'What do you mean?'

'You came up with Dead Straight Line.'

'Never copyrighted it but, okay, it was my idea.'

'Well, it seems your idea has indeed been copied, many, many times.' Mr Thomas goes to his laptop and turns it to me. 'Watch this.'

He presses play. It's a clip from TikTok. Someone's holding a camera and moving across a garden at night. Hear laughter, muffled voices and heavy breathing. Sounds like some young lads messing about. They come to a fence. The shot goes wobbly as whoever's holding the camera hurtles over the top and lands with a heavy crash on the other side. More laughter.

'It goes on,' he says, taking the laptop back and pressing pause.

'They're doing Dead Straight Line?'

'Yes.'

'What's it got to do with me?'

'Unfortunately, it's got a lot to do with you. You've inadvertently started a trend, Rory. What you saw there is not an isolated incident. We've had dozens of reports like this. I've spoken to other headteachers. It's happening with pupils from schools across the area. It's becoming an epidemic.'

Both proud, and whatever the opposite of proud is. The game was only meant to be a bit of fun; fill in a boring evening. Never planned on it going viral. But isn't that what everyone wants nowadays? Global fame.

'I've had messages from parents saying their children are coming home bloodied and bruised, with torn clothes. Had angry emails from residents who've had their gardens trashed by marauding pupils from our school. Some of them are even turning it into a race, with competing teams.'

Why didn't I think of that?

'Only last week, a twelve-year-old boy from Lincoln College climbed over a fence and fell through a greenhouse. He was badly cut. Lucky not to sever an artery. We don't want anyone else getting seriously hurt.'

'Sorry, Mr Thomas, but what do you expect me to do?'

He loosens his tie. 'We've tried speaking to our students at assembly, put messages in the school newsletter, stuck up posters, but nothing seems to have worked. That's why I'm talking to you.'

'You think I can stop them?'

'Not just you. I'd like you to give a talk to the whole school… with Eliot Hollings.'

FORTY

'YELL?'

'If by that you mean Eliot, then yes.'

'He hates me.'

'I'm not asking you to become friends. I'm asking you to help us.'

Never expected this in my wildest dreams, and some of mine have been pretty insane since I started sleeping again. Mr Thomas is asking me to not only meet Yell, he wants me to stand in front of the whole school and trash Dead Straight Line.

'How many students will be there?'

'About eight hundred, plus teachers and parents.'

The thought sends a shiver on a tour of my body. Only ever spoken in class. Telling so many people how to behave doesn't belong in my skill drawer.

'Why not ask him to do it?'

'Better if it's both of you.'

Can see why. You get the inventor of Dead Straight Line and the victim of Dead Straight Line on the same stage at the same time.

'Have you spoke to Yell— iot yet?'

'No, but I intend to. I wanted to speak to you first, find out if you're up for it.'

'What if he's not?'

'Then we'll go with you.'

'What if I'm not?'

'Then we're back to square one,' he says. Can tell sliding down the snake to square uno is not what Mr Thomas wants.

'There's another problem,' I say. 'His sister Lauren was going out with Shar— Finn. She was behind the attacks on our house.'

Mr Thomas rubs his stubbly chin. 'I understand that Lauren complicates matters, but we needn't involve her in any way. This isn't about his sister; it's about you and Eliot and Dead Straight Line.'

Mr Thomas has cracked my brain open like an egg and scrambled it.

'When do you want an answer?'

'As soon as possible. Only last night there were three more incidents. We're running out of time.'

Can't believe it. The headteacher who threw me out wants me to come back to solve his school's behavioural problems. Even if I did invent the game, I did nothing to spread the word. I'm not an influencer with ten million followers, I'm Rory Gordon, with no friends – apart from Eden – and four social media accounts. All defunct. On top of that, the thought of speaking to all those people makes me want to throw up breakfast, lunch and dinner. What if they start booing, heckling, snoring, laughing? I was fine with my gang of six. But eight hundred, including teachers and parents?

And what if it doesn't work? Like Dr Frankenstein, I'll have created something that's totally out of control. What if it spreads to other towns, cities, countries? Can imagine it reaching America.

News just in. Ten children in Ohio killed after taking a short cut through a nuclear power plant as part of a terrible new global craze... Dead Straight Line.

His request resurrects my anger.

'You threw me out of this school, Mr Thomas, accusing me of throwing Yeliot off that roof. But there was no proof that happened. It was his word against mine. And you chose his.'

He shuffles in his seat, before fixing me with a how-dare-you? stare. 'Eliot was injured in a game *you* created, Rory. *You* were the older boy. *You* should have shown more responsibility.'

'What about his responsibility?'

Mr Thomas's mouth makes a small hole through which a long sigh escapes. 'After what happened we couldn't in all honesty have you and Eliot in the same school. Feelings were running very high.'

'This is all about school image, isn't it, and what are those reports called… Ofcon?'

'Ofsted.'

Mr Thomas mulls.

'I can't deny the reputation of the school is important. Whatever happened on that roof had no bearing on our decision, though. You'd created a dangerous game during which one of our pupils was seriously injured. We have a duty of care to our students.'

'What about a duty of care to me?'

He looks up at the ceiling and then back at me.

'I take it from your tone, Rory, you won't be doing the talk.'

'Correct, Mr Thomas. Goodnight.'

FORTY-ONE

FACETIME EDEN AND tell her about the strange evening in my old headteacher's office.

'That's good isn't it?' she says.

'Which part of it is good?'

'The fact he wants you to help them. Wouldn't do that if he didn't trust you. Trust is important, you know.'

'This is the guy who booted me out of school, Eden. He hated me. Almost as much as I hate him.'

'Maybe his hate has gone. People can change.'

'Not this guy. He wants me to do his work for him. Isn't that what they pay Pastoral Care teachers for? I should charge him. A hundred quid an hour, plus travel expenses.'

'Be sensible, Rory. He's giving you an opportunity… for redemption.'

'I don't need redemption. I've done nothing wrong.'

'You don't call trespassing wrong? You don't call scaring people wrong? You don't call damaging people's gardens wrong? You don't call what happened to Eliot wrong?'

'Whose side are you on?'

Eden looks flustered. 'Your side, of course. But you're not totally innocent.'

'Maybe, but I'm not as guilty as Sharky and Lauren. What happened with Yell was an accident. Everything they did was deliberate.'

'I don't know why you're even talking to me about this, Rory. Seems you've already made your mind up.'

Thought Eden would back me. She's done the opposite.

'What do you think I should do then?'

'Give it some serious consideration. Even if you think you've been badly treated, it doesn't mean you shouldn't do something to help. Two wrongs don't make a right.'

'You think I'm mad, don't you?'

'You're not mad, Rory. You're an idiot – a lovable idiot – and I have Spanish revision to do. Adios.'

'Adios.'

She hangs up.

Why are girls so sensible? Why can't she be stupid for once in her life, and say: 'Yeah, let kids jump through hedges, better than taking drugs.' Eden's not designed that way. She's not a rule breaker. Thinks I should give the talk. But she's not me. I'm the one who has to be on stage and do it, at a school that expelled me.

I need to do some homework, but my brain's not interested. Instead, I lie on my bed, thinking about what Mr Thomas said. Reckon he's exaggerating about Dead Straight Line, the way teachers do. He only showed me one video. Where were all the others? How many gardens have been wrecked? How many kids have been nabbed by the police? How many people have been injured? Teachers always stress the importance of facts. Where are his?

My thoughts are derailed by the sound of voices coming from our back garden. The kids next door must be playing football. Go over to the window and peer out. But it's not youngsters kicking a ball. It's three teenagers I've never seen before, running across our garden, past the blackened patch where the garden shed once stood, to the next-door neighbour's fence.

I open the window and scream at them to clear off. The sound of my voice gives them an extra burst of adrenalin and they fly like wild deer over our fence. I watch as they pelt across next door's lawn and disappear.

Close the window.

Maybe Mr Thomas was right after all.

FORTY-TWO

EDEN AND I put on our masks, gel our hands and walk towards Tanker's ward. I spot a young nurse I've seen a few times before.

'Hi, we're friends of Mr Osborne, or Tanker. How is he?'

Award for stupidest question of the day. He's in hospital. On a ventilator. He's got diabetes. He's lost a leg. She's hardly likely to say he's ready to do a triathlon. But I need to know what's going on.

'Mr Osborne has severe bacterial pneumonia. We've put him on a course of antibiotics. It can clear up within a few days, but he's quite poorly. We may need to keep him on antibiotics for quite some time.'

'And then he'll get better?' asks Eden.

'We hope so. Mr Osborne is very frail. The fact he has diabetes doesn't help. A lot depends on how he reacts. We're monitoring him all the time.'

'He told us he finds it hard to read.'

'Yes, his lungs are struggling. When oxygen levels decrease it can affect your eyesight too.'

'We read to him, but he keeps falling asleep,' says Eden.

'Don't stop what you're doing. Mr Osborne loves you two coming in. He talks about nothing else.

'Sorry I need to go,' she says, and hurries away to deal with someone else whose body is no longer functioning.

Eden and I walk into the ward.

'Hello, Tanker,' I say.

'Eh, who is it? Oh, you twos,' he says, squinting in our direction.

Good to see Tanker. But not in this condition. He looks even worse than before, his breathing short and raspy, like a Disney cartoon villain. His cough, when it appears, is deep and loud, the sort teachers make to grab the class's attention. He's not the sharp guy I first met. Guess that's what age, drugs, diabetes and pneumonia does to you.

'Can we get you anything?' asks Eden.

'Aye, a new body,' says Tanker, coughing something into a tissue. His cough goes on so long seems he's dragging it up from his toes. The five he has left. He slumps back into his pillow.

He finally settles.

Eden elbows me. We'd agreed to ask his advice about the headteacher's request, but not sure he's in any condition to respond.

'Can tell yous two are up to something.'

'Rory has something to say.'

Might as well tell him.

'Need a bit of advice.'

'Divvent drink on an empty stomach.'

Maybe Tanker is still functioning after all.

'My old headteacher called me in. The game I started, Dead Straight Line – the one that injured Yell, that lad you saw – has been copied by loads of kids. Caused a ton of trouble. So he says. Wants me and Yell to talk to the whole school to try to get them to stop. What do you reckon I should do?'

'Got any easier questions?'

Eden and I laugh.

'Let's think,' he says, scratching the back of his scrawny hand, the one without the cannula. 'You've said yersel, you wish this lad hadn't hurt hisel. If you talk to the school mebbes these kids will stop.'

'What if it goes wrong? Like them ignoring me, laughing at me.'

'Then at least you've had a go. Like I said before, kidda, weigh up the good versus the bad. Whichever comes oot on top, wins.'

Tanker makes it sound so easy.

'But divvent take the word of a daft old gadgy like me. Make your own mind up.'

Tanker starts another of his coughing fits. It's like an internal earthquake that leaves him wheezing, as he stares, wide-eyed at the ceiling.

'Do you want us to call a nurse?' asks Eden.

'Na, this is normal… for me,' he groans.

'Would you like us to go?'

'No, I'd like you to read. Take iz back to the First World War, pet.'

I grab *All Quiet on the Western Front* from his bedside table and we return to the mud and the blood of the trenches. I'm no more than a couple of pages in before Eden elbows me. Tanker's asleep again.

'Better go,' she says quietly.

I touch his hand. Eden pats his arm. We leave the ward, take our masks off and walk out of the hospital towards the bus stop.

'Still got some spirit in him,' says Eden.

Yeah, but it's diluted. He's not the guy I first met.

We reach a busy road junction. The pedestrian crossing symbol turns red. I rush over. Look back. Eden is still on the other side, arms folded, unamused. She waits for the sign to turn green before joining me.

'Why didn't you cross?' I ask.

'Why did you?'

'It was safe.'

'The red man isn't there for decoration, you know,' she says.

'Do you never take risks?'

'I'm going out with you.'

I laugh.

'Why are girls so cautious?'

'Perhaps we want to live a bit longer.'

'But what about the buzz, the excitement?'

'Of being hit by a car?'

'Of running fast and not being hit by a car.'

'Is it really worth it?'

'I got there before you.'

'Big deal. Rules are there for a reason.'

'Maybe, but they're boring.'

'If you want to be a stuntman, Rory, go to Hollywood,' says Eden, elbowing me in the ribs.

We reach her bus stop. Eden kisses me goodnight as her bus pulls up.

'Love you, Mr Rebel.'

'Love you, Miss Road Safety.'

Eden climbs aboard. I watch as she takes a seat, breathes on the window and draws a heart. The bus disappears into the distance. Think about what Eden said. Everywhere you look are risks. Big ones. Small ones. What about the school talk? Is that a risk worth taking? Try weighing up the pros and cons. They both seem to weigh the same. Why is nothing ever simple? A second later it gets a whole lot more complicated.

Feel my phone ping. Take it from my pocket and look at the message. It's from a number I don't recognise.

> Hello, Rory, it's Carol Hollings – Lauren and Eliot's Mum. I'd like to talk to you. Can we meet in the Jumping Beans café after school tomorrow, 5 p.m.? Thanks C.

FORTY-THREE

'HELLO, RORY.'

'Hi, Mrs Hollings.'

'What happened to Carol?'

That's what I used to call her was when I was seeing Lauren. Prefer Mrs Hollings now. Carol makes us sound like friends. We're a billion miles from that.

'Would you like a drink?' she asks, her fingers fiddling with a plastic menu on the table.

'No, thanks.'

Can't believe I'm sitting opposite the woman who was swearing at me a few weeks ago. The woman whose husband was fighting my dad on her front lawn. The woman whose daughter caused massive problems for me and my family. The woman whose son is in a wheelchair, because of my game.

The silence is beyond awkward. Decide to break it.

'How's Yell, sorry, Eliot?'

'Doing as well as we could hope. He's a tough little lad, especially up here,' she says, tapping the side of her head. 'It's a lot for a teenager to have to deal with. Unsure about what the future holds. It's not going to be easy for him. He's been so strong, though. A lot stronger than I've been.'

Didn't get a good look at her on the night of the garden-gnome fight but can tell the impact Yell's spinal injury has had on her. Her face is pale, with deep creases and tired eyes, as if she hasn't slept since the accident.

'I'm sorry,' I say.

She glances down. Think she might be about to cry, but she bites her lip and blinks the tears back. 'It's like the plot twist you weren't expecting. Except this is real. Simple things like getting on a bus or a train are a right palaver. All the things we take for granted, gone in a second. Medicine might be getting smarter the whole time, but you can't rebuild a spinal cord can you?'

She blows her nose.

'And now the stuff with Lauren.' The mention of her daughter is too much for her. She grabs a tissue and wipes her eyes. 'Sorry... Shed enough tears these last few months to fill a swimming pool.'

Feel bad for Mrs Hollings. None of this is her fault. She had two kids, leading normal lives, until I came on the scene. Don't want to put the next question on the table, but sometimes you have to ask, even though you don't care about the answer.

'How's Lauren?'

Takes a while for Mrs Hollings to respond.

'Not good. She's been suspended from school. The Crown Prosecution Service are looking at her case. The idea of her going inside is too horrible to think about. Not after what happened to our Eliot. Even if they don't press charges, it doesn't change what she did, getting that lad to do those things. Why didn't she tell me what she was planning?'

Because you'd have stopped her, and Lauren didn't want that. She needed to see me and my family suffer, the way yours has.

'She loved you, Rory, she really did.'

A love that turned to loathing, in the blink of an eye.

I liked Lauren. But wasn't obsessed with her. I had the gang to keep me occupied when she wasn't around. Guess she only had me. And her little brother. Whom she loved even more.

'Used to go on about you the whole time: Rory this, Rory that. Think it made it ten times worse for her after what happened. Her introducing Eliot to you and your group. She thought you'd be perfect for him. I did too. You were so well-behaved whenever you came around ours. Cheeky, but nice. Had no idea what you and the others were doing.'

Mrs Hollings changes tack.

'How's your mum coping?'

'Okay, now the attacks have stopped. But before I caught Sharky she was in a bad way. On medication. Not sleeping. Wanted us to move.'

'Sorry about the damage and everything.' She blows her nose. 'Send her my regards.'

Not sure Mum will be sending any back.

She looks at a bunch of pupils from my school, crowding around a phone, laughing at the screen. Then she looks at me.

'I've tried to hate you, Rory. I really have. You took everything from us: my boy, my family, our future. I tried blaming Eliot. I tried blaming myself. But it always came back to you. You're responsible for all this.'

Mrs Hollings stares at me, her face streaked with tears.

'But the hate wouldn't stick. Out on those streets you might have been reckless, a rule breaker, bit of a tearaway, but I know deep down you'd never do anything to deliberately hurt our Eliot.'

'You don't believe I pushed him.'

'I don't know what to believe. All I know is my son is going to be in a wheelchair for the rest of his life, and no amount of anger is going to change that. Hate has been eating me up, and I can't take it any more.'

The tears start again.

I reach over and touch her hand. She takes mine.

A few days ago, there was more chance of me walking in flipflops to the South Pole than holding Yell's mum's hand. But here I am, in a café, doing exactly that. Her words lift a weight that's been crushing me.

'There's another reason I wanted to meet you today.'

I sit up straight.

'Mr Thomas, the headteacher, has been on the phone about kids playing your stupid game.'

'He talked about it to me too.'

'He wants you and Eliot to give a talk at school telling them to stop.'

'Eliot's never going to agree to that.'

'That's where you're wrong. Eliot wants to meet you.'

FORTY-FOUR

THE SURPRISES KEEP on arriving. Like junk mail. Impossible to stop.

First Mr Thomas. Then Mrs Hollings. Now Yell. After all that's happened, he's the last person on earth I imagined would want to talk to me.

Know what Mum and Dad will say.

Stay away from that boy. His family are toxic.

Decide to ask someone who's not been poisoned by what's happened.

I'm on my own tonight at the hospital. Eden's gone to see her gran who's having her eighty-ninth birthday party.

'The lad in the wheelchair wants to see yous?' says Tanker slowly, as though each word is a bit of gristle that needs chewing over.

'Yeah, what should I do?'

'I'm an old soldier, man,' he replies. 'I'm not King Solomon.'

'Who's he?'

'Clever gadgy, wise as a weasel.' Tanker looks up at the ceiling as he thinks. 'Let me ask yous something. Between you and this lad, who's sufferin' the most?'

Only one winner. Didn't need Yell's mum to remind me what he's facing. My Google search history consists of *'wheelchair users', 'spinal injuries', 'problems for wheelchair users', 'helping paraplegics walk again', 'jobs for people in wheelchairs'.*

'Yell.'

Tanker nods. 'You'll recover; his legs won't.'

He's right. Despite his lie, my life will go on pretty much as before. One day I'll move from this town and meet people who have no idea who I am or what I did. I can escape the past. Unlike Yell.

'What's the verdict?' wheezes Tanker.

'I'll go and see him.'

'Giz your hand.'

I hold it out. Tanker squeezes it as tight as he can. 'Even if it gans badly, you'll have done your best.'

Then, from the depths of his diaphragm, he produces a horrible, hacking cough that reverberates around the ward.

'You okay?' I ask.

'Never been better.'

On the bus home, I text Mrs Hollings and tell her I'll meet Yell. She messages straight back.

Great Let's meet at Copsem School, 6pm tomorrow, C.

*

'Where are you going?' asks Mum, as I grab my coat.

No point lying. She'll track my phone and wonder why I'm going back to the school I no longer go to.

Deep breath.

'Going to see Yell.'

Mum's eyes narrow. 'Eliot Hollings?'

Nod to confirm she's heard correctly.

'What's brought this on?'

Know she won't be happy with what comes next.

'I met his Mum.'

She grips the edge of the table. 'When?'

'Couple of days ago.'

'Is that when you were at the café?'

Nod.

'Thought you were with Eden. Why didn't you tell me?'

'Knew you wouldn't like it.'

'Too right I wouldn't. After what they've done to us.'

'She wants to move on. She's had enough of hating.'

'Well, I'm not sure I have. She must have known what that hideous daughter of hers was up to. Wouldn't be surprised if she was involved herself.'

The hatred Mrs Hollings has shaken off is still deep-rooted in Mum. Maybe there's a hate-by-date, when it will finally wear off.

'Don't fall for her moral blackmail, Rory. Eliot's dad attacked *your* dad. Eliot said *you* pushed *him*. Lauren tried to kill *us*. Why should you believe anything her mum says? Why would you want anything to do with any of that awful family?'

'What about what I've done to them?'

Mum doesn't reply.

'She knew what Lauren was up to,' she says. 'She had to.'

'You didn't know what I was up to.'

Mum's eyes fill with tears. 'Have you any idea how much that hurts me, Rory? That I didn't pay enough attention to what you were doing. That I didn't ask enough questions. That I wasn't curious about my own son. Maybe when you're a parent, you'll realise.' Mum looks outside at the scorched patch of earth where our garden shed stood. 'As for that woman. She thinks you can turn over a new page just like that, does she?'

'I don't know what she thinks, Mum, but she doesn't want things to stay the way they are.'

'I'm not a vengeful person, Rory, but that family...'

Her tear glands go into full production. I give her a hug.

'I need to see him. I want to see him.'

Mum composes herself.
'Go then. Seems you do whatever you like anyway.'
'Thanks, Mum.'
'I'll come with you.'
'No.'
'But what if it's a trap?'

FORTY-FIVE

I CATCH THE bus on my own, Mum's words on repeat in my head.

What if it's a trap?

Lauren could have used her Mum to lure me to my old school. Unlikely, but then it was beyond belief she'd use Sharky to carry out those attacks. What if her cousin, Andy is back from the army? Could she have recruited him too? What if Mrs Hollings's words are as fake as the stories on social. Could this be a final act of revenge?

The thoughts that kept me awake last night, are still here today, messing with my temperature gauge, turning my heart into a tom-tom drum. Considered asking Eden along, but if things turn nasty, she's the last person I want involved. I wear my old Dead Straight Line trainers, in case running is the only option.

Get off the bus and walk to Copsem High, checking for anyone that looks suspicious. But everyone looks normal. Apart from me. Head down, sneaking looks this way and that. Reach the school. Only four cars in the car park. Look up at a CCTV camera that's been well and truly smashed. Walk towards reception, my head in meerkat mode, looking in all directions for possible danger. I reach the main doors and go inside. Spot Yell and his mum.

Fear grips me.

Realise it's not only an attack I'm scared of. It's meeting Yell.

Come on, Rory, you can do this.

Walk slowly towards them.

'Hello, Rory,' says his mum.

'Hi, Mrs Hollings. Hi, Yell.'

'His name's Eliot.'

Great start.

'Sure. Hi, Eliot.'

Decide to bury Yell. He's Eliot from now on.

'Hello, Rory,' says Eliot, staring at me blankly.

'Is there anyone else here?' I ask, my eyes on full swivel mode.

'The school janitor. Maybe a couple of teachers.'

'No one from your family?'

'Why would they be here?'

Shrug.

Mum had me totally spooked. I guess when your house has been under attack it pays to be twitchy.

'Mr Thomas has given us Classroom 1R,' says Mrs Hollings.

She pushes Eliot down a corridor, opens the door to 1R and wheels him inside. Remember this place from my time here. Got detention for chucking Jason Ritchie's backpack out of the window.

'Do you want me to stay with you, sweetheart?'

'I'm okay,' mumbles Eliot.

'I'll leave you to it then,' she says.

Mrs Hollings leaves the class and closes the door. I grab a chair and sit opposite Eliot. Don't want to be looking down at him or have him looking up to me. Can't believe this is the first time I've had a proper chance to talk to Eliot since I watched him being carried away on a stretcher into an ambulance all those months ago.

So much has happened since then. Nearly all of it bad.

My mind flips into 'what if?' mode. What if we'd stayed in that night? Eliot would be walking, Lauren and I would still be going out, our front window would be in one piece, the garden shed would be standing, all my clothes would be in my wardrobe and our car wouldn't have needed a new paint job. The only thing that would have changed would be the gang. They'd made it clear that they wanted nothing more to do with me.

Eliot and I sit there like strangers on a train, aware of each other, but eyes desperately searching for something else to land on. It's not just our eyes that are affected. Our tongues are too. There are thousands of words in the dictionary, but we can't find a single one to get the conversation going. I could talk about Eden. But if it gets back to Lauren it will only make a bad situation even worse. Me finding a new girl, while she's lost me, Sharky and maybe even her freedom.

Eliot breaks the silence.

'Thanks.'

'For what?'

'For coming.'

I smile, and our eyes agree to meet.

Hope this goes better than our last meeting.

'Who was that woman with you in the mini supermarket?'

'My Aunty Esther. Sometimes visit her. Her house has more space than ours. She went a bit crazy, didn't she?'

'Yeah, she did.' Lean closer to him. 'I'm sorry, Eliot, so sorry.'

He nods.

'Wish I hadn't asked you to play that game. Could tell you didn't want to do it.'

'But I did,' he says, gripping the wheels of his chair. 'I wanted to prove myself to you and the others. You'd all done it. I didn't want to be left out. Didn't want to be a coward.'

'You weren't. I never wanted to involve you in anything dangerous, Eliot. Nothing had ever gone wrong before. Apart from Mad getting bitten on the arse by a dog and Dean falling into a pond. Wouldn't have done it if I thought it was so risky.'

Risk is the snake that bites when you least expect it. You think of the nine hundred and ninety-nine times out of a thousand when everything goes right. You never consider the time when it might go wrong.

Until it happens.

'The roof was high.'

'Yeah, it was,' I say. 'Should have looked for another way out. Should have shone my phone into that garden. Should have lowered you down. Should have done lots of things.'

Struggle to find the right words.

'Your mum says you've been... brave.'

'What else is there to be?'

Eliot makes it sound easy, as if bravery is something you can put on and off, like a coat. I know that's not true. When I think of my so-called friends, none of them found the courage to speak to me. Cowardice is the easier coat to wear.

Decide to find a bit of bravery of my own. Have a question for him. He won't like it. Need to ask it, though. Grip the edge of my chair.

'Why did you lie about me?'

Eliot looks at his legs and rocks his wheelchair backwards and forwards. Backwards and forwards. Backwards and forwards.

Sense he's not going to say anything.

But he does.

'I was angry about what happened, Rory. Would never have been up there on that roof but for you.'

'I could have gone to prison.'

'I know,' he says. 'The lie got out of control. And the longer it went on, the harder it was to backtrack. What was I gonna say: "you know I told you Rory pushed me off the roof? Made a mistake, it was me that jumped"?'

'You got me thrown out of school.'

'You're not missing much.'

I laugh.

He's right. I look around. Copsem's not the best place, and if I hadn't gone to Hayford would never have met Eden.

'Will you ever change your mind about the lie?'

Eliot looks outside and shakes his head. He knows if he talks, there'll be repercussions. The trouble will be dug up all over again. People may like me a little bit more, and like him a little bit less.

If I was in his shoes, would I do the same?

Maybe.

Probably.

Definitely.

'Does Lauren know we're meeting?'

'Yeah, Mum told her. She went batshit crazy. Said I was siding with the devil. Said she'd never speak to me again.'

'Lucky you.'

A miniscule smile on Eliot's face. Then it's gone.

'What about your dad?'

'Didn't want me to meet you either, but he said I'm old enough to make my own decisions.'

Eliot is no longer the pushover I thought he was. Imagine the fighting that went on in his house just so he and his mum could come here tonight.

'Why did you want to see me?' I ask.

'It's about the school talk. I want to do it.'

'Why?'

His fingers run back and forth along the curve of the wheels. 'Spoke to Mr Thomas. He told me what's happening out there with your game. Don't want anyone else to go through what I have.'

'Chances are nothing will ever happen.'

'It happened to me.'

He's right. Remember that only last week a kid fell through a greenhouse and nearly killed himself. You can't trust chances.

'What about you?' he asks.

Look outside, half expecting to see a bunch of kids vault the school fence, taking the difficult route home.

DEAD STRAIGHT LINE

I look at Eliot, in his wheelchair.
It's time to put a stop to Dead Straight Line.
'Yeah, I'll do it.'

FORTY-SIX

I PACE UP and down as Eliot wheels himself back and forth. We're both as nervous as high-board divers, steeling ourselves for a leap into the unknown, praying the jump is a good one. I've spoken in class before, but never to this many pupils, teachers and parents. To ratchet my nerves even higher the crowd includes Eliot's mum and dad, my mum and dad and Poppy. That is way too many eyeballs.

Glad Eden isn't here to watch me make a fool of myself.

Mr Thomas was over the moon when he heard Eliot and I were up for talking. The news flew straight into the school newsletter, which he forwarded to me.

I'm delighted to announce that on Thursday at 4.30 p.m. there will be a talk from myself, Chief Constable Battersby, former pupil Rory Gordon and Eliot Hollings (Y10) about the dangers of the latest craze – Dead Straight Line. All pupils are requested to attend. Parents and siblings are welcome.

Kind regards,
Mr Thomas
Headteacher

Eliot and I watch from the side of the stage. Fortunately, from where I'm standing, I can only glimpse one per cent of the crowd. If I could see everyone, I'd run away faster than Barny chasing a bus. Wonder if anyone's ever died of stage fright.

'Are you ready?' asks Mrs Layne, the deputy head.

'Yeah,' we both lie.

Eliot looks every bit as nervous as me.

Mr Thomas and the Chief Constable walk out on stage. Their appearance presses pause on the chattering.

'Hello, everyone,' says Mr Thomas. 'Glad so many of you could be here this afternoon to discuss a topic that's risen as rapidly as a hot air balloon to the top of the school agenda. I'm talking about the game called Dead Straight Line. It sounds harmless enough…'

… apart from the word Dead…

'… but it can have terrible consequences. Which we'll come on to later.'

My eyes avoid Eliot, who I'm sure is looking at me.

'I wouldn't normally call a meeting like this, but this particular game has got out of hand. As I'm sure you're aware, it involves young people getting home in a straight line through the gardens of total strangers. It's a very silly, very juvenile, very stupid and potentially a very dangerous thing to do.'

You could toast marshmallows on my cheeks. Here I am, the inventor of the very silly, very juvenile, very stupid, potentially very dangerous game.

'I've had numerous calls and emails from both parents and local residents who've been affected by what's going on. They are worried about the damage being caused to their children and their properties respectively.

'We aren't the only school in the area to be affected. I've spoken to the headteachers of Hayford Free, Lincoln College, Rayling High and Benton Boys. They've all had similar issues and are deeply concerned about what's going on. On that note I'd like to hand over to Chief Constable Mike Battersby.'

The Chief Constable, a giant of a man, walks to the front of the stage and takes the microphone. 'Thank you, Mr Thomas,' he says, in a voice that booms across the hall. 'I'm normally called into schools to talk about the dangers of drugs, zombie knives, alcohol abuse, road safety or sexting. It's not often I'm called in to talk about gardens.'

Smattering of laughter from the audience.

'But this is a serious business. Going into someone's property is trespassing. Destroying something that belongs to another person is criminal damage. What may seem like a bit of harmless fun can lead to a criminal record. On top of that, pupils need to think about the effect of their actions on others. We have a high percentage of elderly in this borough. Imagine you're an old person, at home, late at night. You hear the voices of young people in your garden. You don't know they're passing through. You assume they've come to your property to break in and rob you. You're incredibly afraid and call 999. This has happened many times. Of course, when officers turn up, the young people have long gone. But the damage has been done. The elderly residents are often traumatised by the intrusion. Would you want that to happen to your grandma or grandad? I imagine not.

'I'm all in favour of young people getting out, having fun, but not when it comes at the expense of causing fear and harm to the residents of our community. On top of that there is the risk young people are taking. Residents may wish to defend their property with barbed wire or guard dogs. They are well within their rights to protect what's theirs. Young people are at risk of serious injury if they attempt to enter such a property. You may be aware that a young lad from Lincoln College recently fell through a greenhouse while attempting the game. He was badly injured and came close to severing an artery, which could have proved fatal. We don't have the resources to patrol every street. We need to focus our attention on serious crime. We need to stop Dead Straight Line.'

Polite clapping from the crowd as the Chief Constable hands the microphone back to Mr Thomas and steps to the side.

'Thank you so much, Chief Constable. Very wise words, which hopefully will resonate with every young person in this room.'

Mr Thomas then looks at me and Eliot. Never mind the fear of jumping into someone's garden, what about the trauma of going on stage in front of eight hundred people? My heart is thumping so fast, there are no gaps between the beats. It's one long noise.

'I'd now like to invite two students on stage. Can you give a big hand, please, to Rory Gordon and Eliot Hollings.'

FORTY-SEVEN

EVEN FROM UP here I can see eyebrows arching and mouths forming perfect 'o's as we appear from the side of the stage.

Rory, the pusher, and Eliot, the pushed.

Together.

Always thought it must be great to be in a band in front of a cheering audience. Now I think I'd rather be in the crowd. My mouth is so dry there's not enough saliva to sing a note. My brain is frazzled to the point I couldn't play the simplest chord. I'd be booed off stage.

I'd agreed with Mr Thomas and Eliot that I'd talk first. Why did I do that? If I'd gone second, I could have listened to what Eliot had to say and prepared my piece. Could have grown used to all those faces staring up at me. But here I am. Alone in the spotlight.

Mr Thomas hands me the microphone. 'There you go, Rory.'

I take it in my sweaty palm and look out.

There, in the second row, I spot Mad, Dean and Barny, each with an expression of contempt on their face, willing me to fail, willing me to fall.

'I...'

What comes next?

Words, Rory, they want words.

'I'd like to...'

What would I like to? Oh, yes.

'I'd like to thank Mr Thomas for inviting me back today.'

Look down at a sea of disinterested faces. So, this is what it's like being a teacher.

'My name is Rory.'

Idiot. They know that already.

'And I invented Dead Straight Line.'

Invented? Makes me sound like Thomas Edison.

The Nobel Prize for Keeping Teenagers Occupied goes to...

'I didn't mean to create it, it just sort of happened.'

What is coming out of my mouth? Should have written some notes and read from them. Used to be brim-full of confidence, but the school hall has pulled the plug on that and drained every last drop.

'The game was meant to be a bit of fun. But it didn't end up that way.'

A bead of sweat escapes down my neck.

'Why did we do it? Me and my friends were bored. We didn't have much money. We wanted a bit of excitement, something that didn't cost anything. That thing was Dead Straight Line.'

Look at the faces. Blank. Like opening a new Word doc. Have no idea if they like what I'm saying or would rather be having a tooth extraction without anaesthetic. Poppy will tell me later.

'We didn't mean to scare anyone. The idea was to scare ourselves.'

Laughs.

'It was like a rollercoaster, one you didn't have to queue for. We didn't want to damage anything. Most of the damage was to our clothes... Sorry, Mum.'

Can't see her, but know she's out there in the crowd, probably wishing she'd stayed at home, ironing.

'I didn't mean for it to catch on. It was just a silly game. Until it stopped being silly.'

Look at Eliot, who's staring down at his legs.

'One night the game went wrong. Badly wrong. I'll hand over to Eliot to tell you what happened.'

Give the microphone to him.

'Thanks, Rory.'

Eliot puts the microphone in his lap and wheels himself to the middle of the stage.

Never heard silence like it.

A little cough, then he starts. 'My name's Eliot Hollings and I'm an example of what Dead Straight Line can do to you.'

No amount of talks or posters or emails could have the effect Eliot has on the audience. He's the living embodiment of repercussions. Everyone sits up straight. They're gripped. Can't see a single pupil on their phone.

'I joined Rory's gang to get out of the house, make some new friends, have some adventures. Got more adventure than I wanted.'

Smiles ripple like a Mexican wave across the room.

'I was scared by some of the things Rory and his gang did. They were a bit crazy. Never done things like that before. But to be in the gang I knew I had to take part. Rory asked me to play a new game. The idea was to head back to my house, in a dead straight line, through different front and back gardens. I was super scared. But didn't want to let Rory or the gang down.'

Eliot is so much better at this than me.

'It was sort of okay to begin with. Terrifying, but okay.'

Find a pin-sized drop of saliva to swallow. Know what's coming next.

'Then we came to this big house. We couldn't find a way out through the back. Massive hedges everywhere. But there was a garden room. Rory said we should climb on the roof, and leap into the garden behind. We pulled over a table, and I climbed up. It was really high. And really dark. I couldn't see a thing.'

'Then it happened... I ended up in the next-door garden. Didn't realise there'd be a big pile of rubble. Landed badly on my back. Couldn't feel my legs. Couldn't get up. I was screaming in pain. Rory climbed down. The people from the house ran out. Ambulance came. I got taken to hospital.'

Can tell the memory is messing with him, but Eliot soldiers on.

'I hoped it would be a broken leg. But it was a lot worse than that. I'd damaged the nerves in my spine. I'm now a paraplegic. Can use my arms, but not my legs. If there are any biology students here, I damaged my spine in the middle, between the thoracic nerves, numbers one to six. The top half of me is fairly functional. The bottom half, not so good. My bowel and bladder don't work like they used to. I've got some equipment that helps me with that. But the main thing is, I'll never walk again.'

See a couple of teachers in the front row wipe their eyes.

'In some ways I was lucky. There were people at the Spinal Cord Injury Centre who'd damaged the nerves at the top of their spine. Quadriplegics. They can't dress or feed themselves. Can't speak normally. Some of them can't even breathe unaided. If I'd fallen differently, that might have been me.

'People have been really kind. I'd like to thank everyone at the centre, all the doctors, nurses, physios, counsellors. Also like to thank my mum and dad. Sorry I've put you through all this. You've been amazing.'

A sob breaks from a mouth somewhere in the hall.

'If we'd gone home by the pavement I'd have walked here today. Don't be like me. Don't do Dead Straight Line.'

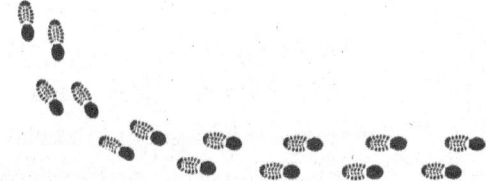

FORTY-EIGHT

CLAPPING ERUPTS.

People get to their feet.

Eliot is the star of the show. He looks over at me, grinning. I give him the thumbs up. Not sure I could come out on stage in a wheelchair and explain what happened to a hall full of strangers. Thought Eliot was a coward. But he's so much braver than me.

'Thank you, Eliot, you were incredible,' says Mr Thomas, patting him on the shoulder. 'So proud to have you as one of our students here at Copsem.'

Unlike the guy standing next to him.

'Before we all head off home, I'd like to open up the room for a short Q and A. Has anyone got any questions for myself, Chief Constable Battersby, Rory or Eliot?'

A dozen or so hands pop up, as if there are puppeteers on the roof.

Mrs Fletcher, my old biology teacher hurries over to a young boy and hands him a microphone.

'Question for Rory,' says the boy. 'Did you think someone might get injured playing your game?'

Mr Thomas hands the microphone to me.

'No, I didn't think it was dangerous. We were chased by dogs, got cut scrambling over walls and through hedges. One of us got soaked, falling in a pond. But that was it. If I'd thought there was a serious risk, we wouldn't have done it.'

Want them all to know it wasn't just me.

Look down at Mad, Dean and Barny.

They all turn away.

'And if I might butt in there,' says Chief Constable Battersby, taking the microphone from me. 'It's extremely important when considering any risk to err on the side of caution. Some of you here today might not wear a helmet when cycling or bother to put on your seat belt in a car. You probably think the chances of anything going wrong are very slim. Which is true. But in my job, I see the result of those who've thrown the dice and lost. The head injuries, the shattered bodies, the deaths from road traffic accidents. You have one life. Cherish it.'

'Wise words, Chief Inspector,' says Mr Thomas as he takes the microphone from him. The head looks out at the waving hands. 'Yes, the lady in the blue coat, near the front.'

One of the mums takes the microphone.

'Question for you, Mr Thomas,' she says. 'What is the school going to do about this problem?'

'Um, yes, very good question.

'The school takes this issue very seriously. And we'll be looking at things we can do to help.'

'Like what?'

'Well, as you know, change takes time. We need to follow due process and run any proposals past interested partners, the school governors, etcetera.'

'Typical,' she moans.

'Any other questions,' says Mr Thomas, keen to move on from the woman in the blue coat. 'Young man over there, with the blond hair,' he says, pointing.

Mrs Harding, who teaches geography, hurries over to the guy, who takes the microphone.

'Question for the Chief Constable.'

He strides forward confidently and takes the microphone from Mr Thomas.

'Fire away.'

'We got burgled a few weeks back, but the police never did a thing. What do you do all day?'

Laughs across the hall.

Mr Thomas grabs the microphone back. 'I don't think that's the standard of question we expect at Copsem. Sorry about that, Chief Constable. Another question, please.' He scans the waving arms and picks out a young woman in the front row.

'Young lady at the front.'

Mrs Fletcher moves down the centre aisle and finds the pupil with her hand up. It's Sadie, the girl whose party I ran from.

'Question for Rory,' says Sadie, staring at me.

Mr Thomas hands me the microphone.

'Why did you push Eliot off the roof?'

Gasps across the room.

What do I say? That I didn't push him, and embarrass Eliot in front of all these people, his mum, his dad, or save his blushes and admit to something I didn't do?

'You don't need to answer that, Rory,' says Mr Thomas.

'Can I answer?' shouts Eliot.

'Are you okay with that, Rory?' says Mr Thomas.

No. But better he carries on with his lie, than I have to deliver a truth no one believes.

'Sure.'

I hand Eliot the microphone.

He looks at me. His face is expressionless. What is he going to do? Bury me once again, in front of all these people?

Then Eliot says the last thing I ever expected to hear.

'Rory didn't push me off the roof. I jumped.'

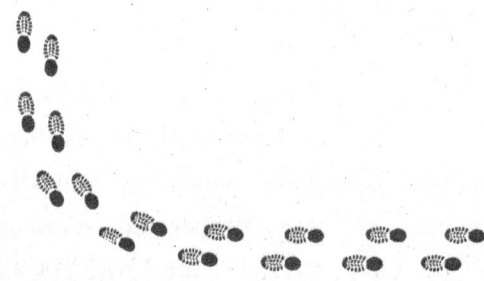

FORTY-NINE

THE COLLECTIVE INTAKE of breath is so sharp you could cut yourself.

Eliot has finally told the truth.

In front of the entire school. His family. My family.

Mr Thomas goes over and kneels next to him. 'Are you sure you don't want to reconsider your answer, Eliot?' he whispers.

'No,' Eliot replies, gripping the microphone tightly, in case Mr Thomas tries to grab it from him. Eliot looks out into the crowd again. 'I said he pushed me because I was angry about what happened. But Rory didn't put the rocks there. He didn't make me jump. He didn't push me. I lied.' He looks over at me, his face crumpled with the pain of his revelation. 'I should never have said it. I'm sorry, Rory.'

Mr Thomas finally manages to wrestle the microphone from Eliot.

'Well, I think we've had enough questions for today. I'd like to thank Chief Constable Battersby, Eliot and Rory, for being here. I hope you've found the presentation interesting and have a deeper understanding of the risks involved in Dead Straight Line. I wish you all a good evening.'

As the crowd begins to head for the exits, I rush over to Eliot, bend down and put a hand on his shoulder.

'Thanks.'

Mr Thomas towers over us. 'Why didn't you tell me this earlier, Eliot?' he says, in his best headteacher voice.

'I was scared,' says Eliot. 'The lie got out of control. My sister said I had to stick to the story. But after what happened with her and Sharky and Rory's family, I knew it was wrong. And when I saw my mum out there and all those people waiting for the answer, I decided it was time for the truth.'

For once, Mr Thomas seems lost for words. He looks at his highly polished shoes, shaking his head. He finally looks at me.

'I'm sorry, Rory.'

Angry and relieved in equal amounts. I've had to live with the lie and its consequences, but I can finally breathe knowing Eliot found the courage to lay the lie to rest.

I stand up and eyeball Mr Thomas. 'You wanted to believe Eliot, and not me. You couldn't bear the fact this was just an accident. You needed a scapegoat.'

'I said I'm sorry.'

What use is that? Is he going to invite me back to Copsem? Are my friends going to forgive me? Is Lauren finally going to come to her senses and realise the enormity of what she's done?

The answers are no, no and no.

I see three members of my old gang making the slow shuffle out of the hall. I grab the microphone from Mr Thomas.

'Mad, Dean, Barny,' I shout. 'See that is what happened that night. I didn't push him. At least Eliot had the guts to own up to it. Unlike you... scum.'

'Please,' says Mr Thomas.

I'm not done yet.

'Before everyone goes home, I want to say something.'

People stop in their tracks.

Eight hundred heads turn to look at me.

I'm not scared any more. I'm emboldened by what Eliot has said.

'It takes courage to tell the truth. But it takes even more courage to admit to a lie. I don't want any of you to criticise Eliot. He's been through enough. What I do want is to send a message to all the students out there. Don't listen to the gossip, the rubbish, the rumours, the lies, the half-truths you find on social media, in the playground, in the classrooms. Don't take sides when you aren't one hundred per cent sure what really happened.

Question everything you hear. And if you don't know, don't judge.'

I hand the microphone back to Mr Thomas. He switches it off. It's caused enough damage for one day.

I go over to Eliot and hug him tight.

'I've ruined everything,' he says, as he bites his lip.

'No, you haven't. You've done the best thing ever.'

I look at the badge on Eliot's blazer.

Veritas.

Truth.

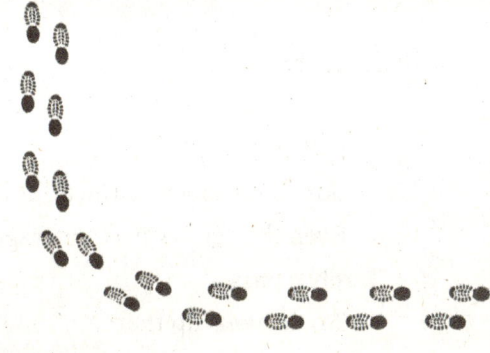

FIFTY

FACETIME EDEN.

'Eliot was lying?'

'Don't look so surprised, Eden.'

I'd told her a thousand times I didn't push him. Maybe I should have made it a thousand and one. Eden seems even more shocked than me by the news. Look across the car park and watch as Eliot's mum and dad lift him from his wheelchair and place him in their car.

'You didn't genuinely believe I'd do something like that?'

''Course not.'

She doesn't say it with the sort of conviction I was hoping for.

'You must feel dead pleased… Eliot saying it in front of all those people.'

'Yeah. And no. Wish it hadn't taken so long to say those two words.'

I jumped.

'Anyway, how was the talk? Bet you were great.'

Even though I wasn't. Average at best. Forty per cent. Barely a pass.

'So nervous up there.'

'Can't believe Rory Gordon is scared of anything.'

Maybe Eden doesn't know me as well as she thinks.

The crowds start to disperse. Imagine they've got a lot more than they bargained for today: a talk, a confession, plus a rant from an ex-pupil. It will be the talk of the school for a few days, going round and round like a relay race, until everyone gets bored with it and some other story becomes the baton.

Hear footsteps.

Turn to see a guy in a Copsem school uniform, eyes firmly fixed on the ground.

Dean.

'I'm gonna have to go, Eden. Call you later.'

'Love you.'

'Love you too.'

End the call.

Turn to Dean.

'What do you want?' I grunt.

'To apologise.'

'Apology rejected.'

His eyes are still glued to his shoes.

'Why didn't you back me up, Dean? How come you believed Eliot, instead of the guy who was supposed to be your friend?'

'Nobody knew what happened that night,' he mumbles.

'I did.'

Bet Dean's regretting coming over to talk.

'What difference does it make? I hear you all hated me anyway.'

'It's not like that.'

'What is it like?'

His eyes finally find mine.

'Sharky and Barny weren't happy with how things were going, but me and Mad never hated you. Sometimes went a bit far with the games, but we liked you. You were a good laugh. Always livened things up. That's why we hung around.'

'Why didn't you tell me any of this?'

Dean fidgets with the sleeve of his blazer. 'Things were getting so heated over Dead Straight Line. Police interviewing us. Parents wanting us to avoid you. People talking about us at school. Thought it best to keep away.'

'Best for whom? You never messaged me. Never came around my house. Nothing. As if I didn't exist.'

Dean could not have looked more guilty if he'd just murdered a judge in front of a jury.

'We all met up after Eliot's accident. Agreed not to get in touch.'

'And now you're breaking the rules, getting in touch.'

'I'm sick of them telling me what I can and can't do,' he says. 'Sharky's gone, and I'm not letting Barny rule my life. I'm sorry, Rory.'

I want to forgive him.

But can't.

Not yet.

'I'll be in touch,' he mutters.

Let's see.

Dean wanders off. I watch him go, shoulders slumped, hands swallowed by his pockets. Maybe I was too harsh. Maybe not. At least he had the guts to admit he was wrong. More than can be said for the others.

Mum and Dad approach. Feel like I'm a priest in a confessional, as people kneel, waiting for forgiveness. They stop in front of me. Look like they've been to the Dean School of Fidgeting.

'Sorry,' mumbles Dad.

'Very sorry, Rory,' goes Mum. 'We should never have jumped to that conclusion. Proud of you today.'

And for once, I'm proud of myself.

Had the guts to stand up there in front of all those people and tell them what I think.

It was a buzz.

One that didn't rip my clothes.

Or cut my hands.

And best of all. Everyone finally knows what really happened.
We find the accused 'not guilty'.
It feels amazing.

FIFTY-ONE

NEXT DAY ELIOT messages me.

He wants to talk.

Arrange to meet outside his house after school. Could have met somewhere else but know how hard it is for him to get places. I cycle there on two fully inflated tyres. My stomach tightens as I turn into Melbourne Street, the site of the Battle of the Dads. Lean my bike against a lamp-post and text Eliot to say I'm here. Wait on the other side of the street. No way am I going near that front door. I can still see the garden gnome underneath their front window. The one that Eliot's dad tried to smash my dad's head with.

A minute or so later, the door opens, and Eliot appears. He wheels himself smoothly down the ramp on to the path. He's wearing gloves to move the outer wheels of his chair. He finds a drop kerb to wheel himself down and, having checked for traffic, makes his way across.

He stops by the side of the road.

'Can you help me?'

Why?

Then I see. There is no drop kerb on this side. We used to clear two-metre-high fences. Now Eliot struggles with a kerb. Wonder how many more obstacles he struggles with every day. I go around to the handles, tip the wheelchair and ease him on to the pavement.

'Thanks. Still getting the hang of this.'

He puts the brake on. I sit on a garden wall so we're at the same height.

'Weird day, yesterday,' he says.

'The weirdest. And you saved the bombshell till last.'

Eliot smiles. He could have drip-fed the news. Tell his parents, then his relatives, followed by his friends, the school. Maybe it was better to get it over with all in one go.

'Why did you want to meet?'

'Mr Thomas wants us to do more school visits. What do you say?'

'Happy if you are.'

'Sure,' says Eliot. 'I won't wait until the Q and A to say what happened, Rory. I'll say it up front.'

Glad to hear it. There will still be doubters out there.

'Also wanted to say sorry.'

'You've said it already.'

'Need to say it again. Should never have done it.'

Smile. And touch his arm.

'I have a question for you. Why did you decide to tell the truth?'

Eliot rubs his finger along the curve of his wheel. 'I didn't plan to, but when the girl asked that question, my heart nearly stopped. Saw you standing there not knowing what to say. If you said you didn't push me, it meant one of us was a liar. It would make a joke of what we were trying to get them to do. And the pressure from Lauren to stick to my story. Couldn't take it any more. Could see what I'd done to you.'

As if I'd done nothing to him.

Look over at his house.

'What did your mum and dad say?'

'Mum was more sad than confused. Dad was more confused than sad. They even themselves out like that. Mum wants me to apologise to your mum and dad.'

'No need, my parents were there. You've said enough.'

'Thanks.'

'What about your sister?'

'Ask her yourself.'

I follow Eliot's eyes.

A car with learner plates appears at the end of the street. It stops outside Eliot's house. Behind the driving wheel sits Lauren. Didn't even know she'd turned seventeen.

Her mum gets out the passenger side, gives me a quick look and heads into the house. Lauren walks over the road towards us. Haven't seen her since that day in the supermarket when Mum released me from house arrest. My feelings towards her are as confused as ever. But judging from the look on Lauren's face, there's only one emotion at home. Fury.

She stops in front of us, arms folded across her school blazer, her face still wearing the look of contempt she wore that day.

'Suppose you're happy now, are you?' she snarls.

I get up from the wall.

'Why should I be?'

'Getting Eliot to tell all those people he jumped. Did you threaten him?'

'Don't be stupid, Lauren. I'm not like you and Sharky. I don't go around threatening people. Eliot made up his own mind to tell the truth.'

'Truth,' she spits. 'Don't believe that for a second. You were in a hurry to get off that roof. That's why you pushed him.'

She's turned into one of those conspiracy theorists. No matter how much evidence they're given, how many facts they're supplied with, how much data they've got, they'd rather believe crap. She probably also thinks the world is flat, the holocaust never happened, all elections are fixed and the moon is made of cheese.

'You're responsible for all this,' she screams.

'Shut up, Lauren,' shouts Eliot. 'You're to blame.'

'Me?' she says, pointing a finger at herself.

'Yes, you. When I was in the hospital, you kept saying it was Rory who pushed me off the roof. You said I couldn't remember the shove because of the trauma of the injury. You went on and on and on about it. Couldn't take it any more. I was tired, drugged up, sick. That's why I said yes. Regretted it as soon as I said it. But it was too late.'

Lauren shakes her head. 'You're rewriting history, Eliot.'

'I'm not. I landed on my back, not my head. I remember what happened, Lauren. I jumped.'

Tears of frustration well up in his eyes. Can't imagine what life must be like for him, living under the same roof as Lauren.

'Suppose you're going to deny anything to do with Sharky,' I say. 'He's going to be locked up because of you.'

'And you don't think I'm in the shit too?'

'What's gonna happen?'

Lauren kicks at an empty crisp packet. 'I don't know. I'm appearing before the youth court.'

Look across at the car with L plates. She must be optimistic. No roads in Young Offenders.

'Why did you have to drag Sharky into this?'

'He didn't need dragging. He hated you, Rory,' she screams.

'But not as much as you. You made him do all that. He would never have done it on his own. You poisoned him. You had no right to take it out on my mum, Dad, Poppy. They'd done nothing wrong.'

'We hadn't done anything wrong either, but look what you've done to us,' she says, staring down at her brother in the wheelchair. 'You've killed our family.'

'I never asked you to get involved, Lauren,' says Eliot softly. 'I'm the one who's in a wheelchair, not you.'

'But you're my brother; my flesh and blood.'

Lauren starts to cry.

Hate her for what she did. But if someone encouraged Poppy to play a stupid game and ended up in a wheelchair, how would I react? Probably the same. Maybe worse.

'Can't believe you two are even talking,' she says between sobs.

'Rory and I are doing roadshows round schools.'

'Saint Eliot and Saint Rory. Never saw that coming.' Lauren blows her nose on a tissue. 'This could have all been so different, Rory.'

Lauren walks behind Eliot and takes the handles of his wheelchair. 'Come on, let me take you home.'

'No.'

She tries to release the brake, but Eliot pushes her away.

'You don't control me, Lauren. I'm staying here.'

She looks daggers at him. 'After all I've done for you.'

'I didn't want you to do anything, Lauren. I just wanted you to be my sister.'

She howls with the pain and frustration of everything that flowed from that night. Eliot wheels himself over and puts an arm around her waist. Lauren bends down and hugs him.

'Oh, Eliot.'

She finally breaks free and glares at me through two tear-filled eyes. 'Your suffering is far from over, Rory.'

Lauren walks over the road and up the ramp to her house. A moment later the front door slams.

FIFTY-TWO

'**HOW IS HE?**' I ask.

'We're keeping him as comfortable as we can,' says the nurse.

The NHS has tons of money, but until someone invents an anti-old-age drug, there's not a lot they can do for Tanker. Mum says when your body starts turning off the lights, nothing to do but close the front door and leave. But I don't want Tanker to go. I've lost enough friends already.

Walk over to his bed and lean in close. 'Hello, Tanker.'

He heaves open an eye, as if it's the weight of a manhole cover.

'It's Rory,' he mumbles.

'Aye.'

His eye swivels around the room. 'Where's your lass?'

'She's playing padel.'

Tanker would normally insert a smart remark here, but all I get from him is a tiny 'Oh'. The drugs and the pneumonia have stolen his vocabulary. Decide to do the talking. His left ear doesn't work too well, so I get as close to his right ear as I can.

'Did what you said I should do. Went for a talk at my old school the other day, to try to stop the kids rampaging through people's gardens. Eliot and I talked about what can go wrong. To scare them off.'

Tanker nods.

Though I'm not one hundred per cent sure he heard.

Shuffle my plastic chair closer to his ear.

'A girl, Sadie, asked why I pushed Eliot off the roof. Didn't know what to say, what with Eliot right next to me and everyone looking at me. But he came to the rescue. Took the microphone and said he jumped. Never seen so many shocked faces. Had a queue of people afterwards waiting to apologise.'

Think I see a smile on Tanker's face.

'Things have taken a turn for the better, Tanker.'

Squeeze his hand.

'Wish they'd get better for you.'

But that's one miracle too many.

'Is there anything you'd like?'

No reply.

'Is there anything you'd like?' I repeat.

'A walk,' he mumbles.

Not sure I can do that. Especially after what happened last time.

'Please, Rory.'

I find a nurse who's busy looking at some charts. 'Excuse me, Mr Osborne says he wants to go for a walk. Can I take him?'

She looks over at him, and then at the window. 'It's not too cold outside. Fresh air will do him good. Don't take him far. Stay in the little garden at the side of reception. It's nice and sheltered there.'

A couple of nurses carefully lift Tanker out of bed and into his wheelchair. They wrap him in a thick blanket. I wheel him towards the lifts. We go to the ground floor and I push him outside into the garden. There'll be no trip to the shops today.

Thankfully, the path is nice and smooth.

'There you go, Tanker, we've escaped.'

I bend down next to him. His lips move, but they're not creating anything meaningful.

'What is it? What do you want, Tanker?'

'Story,' he mumbles.

A story? I'd left *All Quiet on the Western Front* on his bedside table. Eden and I still haven't got through the First World War. Still fifty pages to go. I don't want to have to wheel him all the way back to his ward to get it.

'Story,' he mumbles again.

Mrs Shields always says how good I am at creative writing. Maybe this is my chance to prove it.

'Okay, I'll tell you a story.'

I push his wheelchair around the garden as I try to think of something.

'Once upon a time... No, scrap that.'

Then it comes to me.

'Oscar was a young soldier in the First World War,' I say, as loudly as I can. 'Nineteen years old. He and his pals from his village in Yorkshire had signed up to fight the Germans. They were full of hope and dreams, but a few months later most of them were full of bullets.'

Not sure Mrs Shields would like that bit.

But I do.

'Oscar was battle-weary; afraid. The shelling and the shooting never seemed to stop. He wanted to go home. He wanted to live. There was an extra reason to stay alive. There was a girl back home he liked. Her name was Emily. She used to sell flowers. But now she worked in a munitions factory in Leeds.

'The war dragged on, as wars do. The mud grew thicker and deeper. The shells rose and fell like the sun. Someone said it would all be over by Christmas. But they didn't specify which one. It was Christmas number three when Oscar heard about a big offensive against the German line. Oscar wasn't sure why they bothered. Every time they took some land off the Germans, a few weeks later the Germans took it back again. The land was like a library book. You only ever got to borrow it.

'Oscar's officer briefed him and his men on a plan to take out the enemy positions. They planned to tackle them head-on at first light. Oscar wasn't sure about this. Attacking in a dead straight line would leave them open to the German guns. He suggested that he and a few men should approach by a river that snaked its way far from the battlefield. The officer was uncertain, but what did he have to lose? Their last attack had been a monumental failure.

'Oscar was right. The men who went in a straight line were cut down, but he and those who followed the river found a breach in the German defences and overcame the machine-gun positions.

'Oscar survived the war. He then set his sights on Emily. One problem. Her mother didn't like him, and when he appeared at their house, she said Emily was out and slammed the door in his face. Oscar didn't believe her and went down the alleyway at the side of the house and waited. He finally spotted Emily in the garden, popped his head over the fence and asked, "Will you go out with me?"

'"My that's forward," she said, blushing.

'Oscar had nothing to lose. If Emily didn't want to know him, better he found out now. But Emily was taken by Oscar's forward approach, and she said yes. Six months later, they were married. They had five children. Oscar never talked about the war, but what he did talk about was taking your chances. "If you want something go for it," he would say.'

Not the greatest story ever, but the best I can do on the spur of the moment.

'Did you like it?'

No reply.

I stop pushing, bend down and speak into Tanker's good ear.

'Did you like the story, Tanker?'

His eyes are closed, his head tilted to one side.

Take his hand and feel for a pulse.

Nothing.

Tanker is dead.

FIFTY-THREE

NEVER THOUGHT I'D miss an old Geordie with an uncontrollable beard and an accent as impenetrable as steel. But I do. He listened to me when no one else would. His sense of humour stayed when everything else fell apart. He showed me that no matter how bad things get, you keep soldiering on. I'd hated the idea of going to Mannings to read stories to old people, but now I feel honoured to have met him. I was the last person he saw. The last hand he touched. The last voice he heard. If that's not special, I don't know what is.

Emotions are unpredictable. For so long it was anger. Now something new has taken its place. Sadness.

'What's up?' asks Mum, as she watches me push food around the plate, as if I don't know where to put it. 'Tanker?'

Nod.

She smiles. Know she's proud of me. Said it enough times. Pride won't bring him back, though.

'Spent so long on his own. I don't want his funeral to be the same.'

'We'll be there and Eden will come,' she says. 'I'm sure some people from the care home will pay their respects.'

'Want more than that.'

'But he was a loner, Rory, you said so yourself. You can't magic up friends who don't exist.'

'Must have someone, somewhere.'

Mum puts her knife and fork down. 'Do you know what regiment he was in?'

'3 PARA, I think. I can check.'

Tanker had a drawer full of old military stuff. Had to be something in there about who he fought with.

'Well, when you do, I'll put something on Facebook. I'll say how Mr Tanker...'

'Dave Osborne.'

'Yes, I'll say an old army veteran from the Falklands died recently with no close friends or known relatives. If anyone knows him or would like to pay their respects, they can come to Hadleigh Crematorium next Thursday.'

'Thanks, Mum.'

Mrs Shields and I go back to Mannings and ask if we can take a look at Tanker's belongings. Mrs York is happy to oblige. Along with Hallelujah, we go through everything. In among drawers full of junk we find some old letters. Discover Tanker's old regiment from the Falklands War. I was right. It was 3 PARA. I let Mum and Silicon Valley do the rest.

Hayford let me and Eden have the morning off to go to Tanker's funeral. Mum and Dad also take a break from work to join us.

'You posted the message, Mum?' I ask, adjusting the knot on my black tie.

'Yes, I posted it,' she says, as we drive towards the crematorium. 'That's all we can do.'

Squeeze Eden's hand. I'm nervous again. But it's a good nervous. I want to be my best for Tanker. Written a short speech. Don't want to be stumbling about like I did at Copsem. Even though it's going to be different to the talk with Eliot. This will be in front of a dozen people at most.

Mum turns into the crematorium.

My mouth flops open.

There are hundreds of people milling about outside.

'Are they all here for Tanker?'

'It's the only service at 11 a.m.,' says Dad. 'Yes, they're here for him.'

Mum manages to find one of the last remaining parking spaces and we climb out. Everywhere I look I see men and women wearing medals. Some young, some old. There are also people who look as though they've never even fought a cold but must have heard about Tanker on social media and have come to pay their respects.

A middle-aged man with a walking stick approaches Mum.

'Hello, are you Mrs Gordon?' he says in a cockney accent.

'Yes.'

'Saw your post on Facebook. Had to come today.'

'Did you know Tanker?'

'Never met the guy. I fought in Iraq and Afghanistan. But I know what those guys went through in the Falklands. When I heard Tanker had no one to see him on his way knew I had to come. Us veterans stick together.'

'Have you come far?'

'Colchester.'

Over a hundred miles away.

'Thanks so much for coming,' says Mum.

'Wouldn't have missed it for the world.'

Tanker was right about the camaraderie of the military. Can't imagine any other job where so many people would gather to pay respects to a guy they'd never even met. There isn't enough room in the chapel to hold everyone, and most people will have to stand outside in the cold, listening to the service on speakers.

Mum, Dad, Eden and I enter the chapel and make our way to the front row, where we join Mrs York and

Hallelujah. Get hugs from them. There are a couple of other carers who've brought some elderly residents from Mannings, including Emily, the mountaineer and Scrabble queen. Found out from Mrs York that Tanker had saved up just enough money to pay for his funeral. Told me there was nothing left for anything else.

We watch as four men dressed in black carry Tanker's coffin and place it on a plinth. The coffin is draped with the Union Jack; his old regimental beret has been placed on top. On the plinth is a picture of him from the 1970s in his uniform, looking nothing like the Tanker I knew. Tall, fit, slim, clean-shaven, with both legs intact.

I hadn't a clue what music Tanker wanted for the service. Chatted with Mrs York and Hallelujah. They had no idea either and told me to choose whatever I thought might work. Found an old First World War song, 'It's a Long Way to Tipperary', played by a military band. The music is upbeat, positive, like Tanker himself. Think he'd have liked it.

When the music stops a vicar appears at the front of the chapel. Didn't know it was going to be a religious ceremony. Our family only ever go to church to hear carols. Maybe there's more to Tanker than I realised.

The vicar stands behind a lectern. He has a smile that's not cut and pasted. It's warm and welcoming.

'I'm so glad to see such an amazing turnout today to bid farewell to Mr Dave Osborne, better known as Tanker. Those who knew him at the care home describe him as one of life's true characters, someone whose honesty and spirit shone through every day. Although he had a difficult life, he never lost his sense of humour and his zest for living was an example to all who knew him. He fought bravely for his country in the Falklands War and served in the army for over thirty years. I'm delighted to see so many members of the armed forces here today, to pay their respects to Tanker.

'I'd now like to say a short prayer. God, our shelter and our strength, you listen in love to the cry of your people: hear the prayers we offer for our departed brothers and sisters. Cleanse them of their sins and grant them the fullness of redemption. We ask this through Christ our Lord. Amen.'

He then asks us to say the Lord's Prayer. One section sends a shiver down my spine.

And forgive us our trespasses,
as we forgive those who trespass against us.

Reminds me of all those gardens I went through. Hope they've forgiven me.

'I'd now like to call on Rory Gordon to say a few words.'

Hearing my name sends a jolt through me.

Here we go again.

Eden gives my hand a big squeeze, and I head out of the pew to the front of the chapel. It's not the Copsem school hall, but there are over a hundred eyes on me, and probably two hundred ears outside, waiting to hear what I have to say.

I put my notes on the lectern. Mrs Shields says, 'Writing is rewriting.' That's what I've done with my speech. Been through it so many times I know it off by heart. Although I have to change the opening to reflect what's happened today.

'I'd like to thank you all for coming. I was amazed when our family drove into the crematorium and saw so many people. I know most of you have never met Tanker, but it didn't stop you making the journey here to pay your respects to an old soldier. He'd have been overjoyed. "Belter," he'd have said.

'I only knew Tanker a few months, but it was long enough for him to make a big impression on me, with his deep Geordie accent, his wild beard and his stories. But what I'll remember most about Tanker is his wisdom. He'd had a tough life, dealing with the events he'd experienced in battle. As he told me himself, he didn't have ordinary PTSD, he had complex PTSD. Tanker never did things by half. He moved away from his family in the North East, lost his close friends, lost his leg to diabetes, but his positivity remained intact.

'I've faced some big problems myself this year, and Tanker helped me so much. He believed in me when many didn't. I'd like to say a huge thanks to him for that. Most of all, Tanker showed me the importance of weighing up the pros and cons before making a decision. I came to Mannings to read stories, but most of the time we talked about his life and mine. He was reluctant at first to discuss what had happened to him, but the more I got to know him, the more he opened up. I'm so grateful for that.

'I was there the day he died. Tanker couldn't talk much by then, but he could listen, and as I pushed him around the hospital garden, he asked if I'd tell him a story. Little did I know it would be the last story he'd ever hear. I didn't have a book on me, so I had to make something up. It was a story of a young soldier in the First World War, who showed great courage, like Tanker.

'Tanker probably saw himself as the forgotten soldier, but today he's not forgotten. He'll be remembered for his bravery in battle, his fortitude as he struggled with the issues life threw at him, and his kindness to me.

'I'll miss you Tanker.'

Manage to make it back to my seat before the tears start. Eden puts an arm around me and kisses my cheek. The vicar returns to the lectern.

'Thank you very much, Rory, for those lovely words.' He then pauses, as he prepares for his final piece. 'We thank you, Tanker, for everything you were and all that you gave, and may you now forever rest in peace with the certain knowledge that you were, and always will be, dearly loved and terribly missed. Farewell.'

There's one more piece of music I reckoned Tanker would like. We slowly make our way down the aisle as the sound of a solitary bugle fills the chapel. 'The Last Post'.

I walk outside. The crowd stands in silence. When the bugle stops, people start to approach me.

'Well done, lad.'

'Lovely words.'

'Beautiful send-off. Tanker would have been proud.'

About to head to the car when an elderly woman pushes her way through the crowd and grabs my arm.

'Can I have a word, pet?'

'Who are you?'

'I'm Hilary, Tanker's ex-wife.'

FIFTY-FOUR

HILARY HAS AN accent baptised in the Tyne. She's every bit as Geordie as Tanker.

'Said some canny things aboot wor Tanker, young 'un.'

'Thanks.'

'Wanted to say goodbye,' she says, staring at the ground. 'We were married thirty-two year.'

Another Geordie averse to plurals.

'Had some canny times. Some rough ones too. The rough ones ended up winning. Things got to him. Think it was the war. Carried it aroond with him. Like ammunition. But he wouldn't talk aboot it. That was Tanker, kept everything bottled up. Apart from beer. If Britain had an Olympic drinking team, Tanker would be captain. Had a thirst on him, that man. That's how he got his name. Had his own tankard at the pub. Got called Tankard for a bit. Somehow became Tanker.'

She takes a deep breath. 'Do you mind me talkin' aboot him?'

'No.'

She fiddles with her fingers, bereft of rings.

'He had mental-health problems, but this was before mental health was invented. Neebody talked aboot it back then. Got jumpy at the titchiest thing. At wor lad's birthday party a balloon burst. You'd think it was an atomic bomb. Tanker nearly hit the ceiling. Massive meltdoon, then went to bed. He had nightmares, moods, anger, insomnia. You name it, he had it. Tried to help him, like, really did, but he wouldn't have it. He finally headed doon south. Was berra for all of us. That's what he said.

'Tracked him doon once. Must have been twenty year ago. Turned up at a hostel he was staying in. Didn't gan well. Don't think he hated us. Reckon he hated hisel. Said he was toxic, like mustard gas. Didn't want to drag us all doon. Told iz to stay away. Didn't want to. But I did. Never heard another thing, till me marra in Fenham said she'd seen a post on Facebook about a funeral… for Dave Osborne, alias Tanker. He couldn't stop me then.'

Hilary looks at the crowds milling around. 'Amazing to see so many people here today. Did you organise that?'

'My mum.'

'Bless her.'

Hilary looks at the chapel.

'What was he like… at the end?'

'Happy. But quiet.'

'I should have found him sooner. At least he found you.'

Hilary starts crying. Huge sobs break from her, as if all the heartache and sadness and love she felt for Tanker are finally breaking free. Never hugged a stranger before, but I hug Hilary. Mum comes over, with a worried expression. Not every day you see your son hugging a sobbing woman.

'Is everything okay, Rory?'

'Yeah.'

Hilary breaks away from me and wipes her eyes.

'Is this your son, pet?'

'Yes.'

'You've done a good job with this one. Wish it had been wor Nigel up there talking today.'

'Where is he?'

Hilary shakes her head. 'He's not big on forgiveness.'

Hilary opens her bag and takes out an old purse. She finds two twenty-pound notes and hands them to me.

'Here you are, son. A little something for yous.'

'No, I can't.'

'Yes, you can, Rory,' says Mum sternly.

I take the money.

'Thanks very much, Hilary.'

'Divvent mention it. The least I could dee. Look after yersel.'

Hilary gives me a final hug and hurries away through the crowds. Mum watches her go.

'That was Tanker's wife, wasn't it?'

'Yeah.'

'What did she say?'

'Some other time, Mum.'

She goes off to find Eden, who's chatting to Emily and others from Mannings. Put the money in my coat pocket and touch something I'd forgotten was there. Dash back into the chapel. The place is empty, but for Tanker's coffin. I walk slowly over and touch the wood.

'Got a little something to help you on your way.'

I take the packet of cheese-and-onion crisps and place it on the coffin.

'Tuck in, Tanker.'

FIFTY-FIVE

IT'S BEEN A month since Tanker died.

A lot has happened since then.

I've decided to stay on after my GCSEs. Me and school get on better since the noise around Dead Straight Line died away, and I no longer have the gang to distract me. Also feel I owe it to Mum, Dad and Eden to be known as someone other than the idiot who messed around. If the examiners are in a good mood, I'll study A-level English, business studies and history.

Things are a lot quieter at home since Sharky got caught. Reckon Mum doesn't bother tracking my movements on her phone, Dad actually smiles at me, Poppy no longer has nightmares and Biscuit only barks when it's absolutely necessary. All quiet on the Gordon front.

I still go to Mannings. Didn't want to at first. There was only one Tanker. But Mrs Shields used her mind-altering words on me and said there were people there who wanted to hear my stories. And I could discover theirs. I now read for a woman called Tabitha. She's the total opposite of Tanker. She has no beard, never fought in a war and hasn't touched a drop of alcohol in forty years. But that's not to say she's boring. Tabitha used to be a top-class athlete and ran her own company making children's clothes called Tabi Tots. She sold the company and moved to Spain with her husband, Max. She came back to the UK when he died, to be nearer her daughter and grandchildren. It took six visits to find all this out. There's a story in everyone, but sometimes you need to dig a little to find it.

Sharky was sentenced to four years in Feltham Young Offenders for what he did to our family. Hard to feel sorry for him. He believed the lie Eliot was spinning and the hate Lauren was spewing. Must have thought if he backed down, he'd lose her. But he's lost her anyway. He's got forty-eight months to figure out where he went wrong. Lauren was sentenced to a Young Rehabilitation Order for her part in the attacks on our family. Got two years community service.

Bumped into her a couple of weeks back, cleaning graffiti off a library wall. Lauren's eyes still blazed with anger. Still hates me for what happened. But think the person she hates more than anyone is herself; for introducing her brother to me, for making him lie about that night, and for getting her new boyfriend to do what he did. Maybe she loved me more than I realised, which made the hate even more potent.

No longer speak to Barny or Mad. Reckon I could build one of Mrs Shield's bridges with Dean, but what's the point? I'm in a new gang now. Just the two of us. Me and Eden. Good to know I've finally found someone I can trust.

I see Eliot at our school visits. The talks seem to be working. The number of kids doing Dead Straight Line has gone from a tsunami to a trickle. When we get to the bit about the roof, he always says he jumped. We get on better since the truth came out. He's doing well. Has a Saturday job at a local garden centre, joined a wheelchair basketball team and hangs out with friends from school. Can't believe I ever doubted his courage. He told me his family are on a waiting list for a new council house that's better suited to him getting around. I'll stay in touch with him, as long as he wants to stay in touch with me.

But guilt is a constant companion. Whenever I see someone in a wheelchair I think of Eliot, and that night. I can't change what happened, but there is something I can do. That's why I'm heading out of the house in my running gear, training for a 10K race for the Spinal Injuries Association.

I head off down the street, at a pace my body's not one hundred per cent happy with. My run quickly turns into a trot. To reach the park I have to navigate half a dozen streets. One of them is Dunbar Road. I put in a sudden sprint, then slow down again. Always do that when I reach number 16. The house where it happened. Should be over it by now. Not sure that's possible. Like Tanker's demons, they've taken hold. Doing lengths.

After two laps of the park, my legs have had enough. Time to head back. Avoiding Dunbar Road, I turn into Hardwick Road, where my trainers do an emergency stop. Up ahead I see them. Lauren and Eden. Up close and arguing.

How does Eden even know Lauren? Never introduced them. Go to different schools. And then it hits me like an open-handed slap. I remember where I first saw Eden. I can picture her. In that garden. At Lauren's house. My legs may have stopped, but my heart is beating faster than ever. Feel sick.

Hide behind a bus-stop poster and wait, glancing to make sure they're still there. Their argument finally runs out of steam, like a kettle that's boiled dry. Eden heads my way, while Lauren heads the other. Wait until she's walked past the poster and grab her arm. Eden stares at me, horrified, terrified, mortified and probably a few other ifieds as well.

'When were you gonna tell me?'
'Tell you what?' says Eden, trying to unfluster herself.
'About you and Lauren. What's going on?'

She's always full of words. Today they take a long time to surface.

'Who told you?'

'Your face.'

Her eyes look towards the sky.

'Now I remember where I first saw you. At a barbecue round Lauren's house. What were you doing there?'

Eden looks up at me. Her words are slow, lumbering. 'Lauren and I are friends. I've known her since primary school.'

Your suffering is far from over, Rory.

'What was your plan?'

'It wasn't *my* idea. It was Lauren's.'

'Don't care who came up with it, what was it?'

She looks like a kid in an exam, searching the air for answers.

'What was it, Eden?' I shout.

Her eyes glaze with tears. 'Lauren couldn't believe her luck when she found out you were going to the same school as me. We met up. Said she wanted you to have some of the hurt she was feeling. The plan was to go out with you. Then dump you.'

'Why would *you* do that?'

Eden's nostrils flare as she fills her lungs. 'I knew Eliot. I hated you for what you'd done to him. And Lauren. And her family. I wanted you to suffer the way they have.'

'You believed I pushed him off the roof?'

'Lauren told me Eliot said you did. 'Course I believed him.'

'That's why you got back with me after I ran away from Sadie's party?'

Eden nods.

'Lauren said I needed to start up again.'

Didn't think my head could get any more mashed up, but Eden has managed it. I'm nothing more than a disposable wipe. Something to chuck away once you're finished.

'What were you and Lauren arguing about?'

'You.'

Can't believe what I'm hearing.

'Lauren wanted to know why I hadn't finished with you yet. I lied and said I was waiting for the right moment. But the truth is… there are only wrong moments. I kept putting it off, putting it off. I saw what you'd been through, the way you were with Tanker, that you weren't the monster I thought you were. And when you told me Eliot admitted he'd been lying, I knew I couldn't do it. Kept coming up with excuses to tell Lauren. She was getting sick of them. Said if I didn't do something soon, she'd do it for me. She was going to tell you what I'd done. I begged her not to. But you know what Lauren's like.'

Only too well.

Tears snake down her cheeks.

'I don't want to be part of it any more, Rory. I don't want to hurt you. *She's* the twisted one.'

'You've hardly been straight.'

I knew I had a huge army of haters. Never dreamed for a moment Eden was one of them. She'd wormed her way into my life, not planning to love me, but to destroy me; a Trojan horse dressed in black.

How come I didn't see it sooner? Because I wasn't looking. The clues were there, though. The way she was so keen for us to go out, in spite of what everybody said about me. The fact she wanted us to get back together after I left her at Sadie's party. That she never asked about Lauren, my ex-girlfriend. That she never spoke about any of *her* friends. Her reaction when she heard Eliot had finally admitted I didn't push him.

'You knew about Lauren and Sharky.'

She shakes her head.

'I don't believe you. Remember the night I caught Sharky. The first question you asked me was "how"? You didn't ask "who", because you already knew.'

'Okay, I knew they were seeing each other, but that's all, Rory.'

'Why didn't you tell me?'

'Lauren told me to keep it a secret. I knew you'd go crazy. Had no idea it was them who were attacking you and your family. I thought me dumping you *was* the plan.'

Maybe it's the truth.

If she'd known what they were doing, she'd have warned them I was hiding in the hedge outside my house.

Maybe it's a lie.

She could have warned them, but Lauren made Sharky do it anyway.

'I trusted you, Eden. I thought we were a team.'

Eden wipes her face with her sleeve.

'Forgive me, Rory.'

'Give me one good reason why.'

'I didn't do anything.'

Spit out a laugh.

'You lied to me, Eden. You didn't invite me to Sadie's party because you liked me, you did it because you were planning to finish with me, before we'd even started.'

'But I didn't finish with you, Rory. We got back together, remember? I love you.'

Love. Ha. Not seen much of that lately.

There's a different Eden in front of me. The Eden I saw yesterday was kind, funny, loving. This Eden... I'm not sure about. Now I know how my parents felt about me, discovering the guy they thought they knew was an imposter.

There are two Rorys.

Now there are two Edens.

'I was right to call you intriguing.'

Where I went wrong was underestimating just how intriguing she could be.

'I'm sorry, Rory.'

Shake my head.

'How can I ever trust you now?'

'I don't know, but aren't I worth the risk?'

That word again.

That's what my life's been about: taking risks, rolling the dice, hoping to throw a double six, praying that what might turn bad, turns good. Dead Straight Line wasn't worth the risk. Is Eden?

'Need time to think about that.'

If I finish with Eden, Lauren will have won.

If I carry on seeing her, I will have won.

Or will I?

How can I carry on going out with Eden after what she's done?

I forgave Eliot. Can I forgive her?

She takes a step towards me.

I take a step back.

Not in the touching mood right now.

'See you around?' she asks softly.

I have nothing left to say.

Eden turns and walks slowly away, head down.

I watch until she disappears from sight.

I could finish with her this second.

Or I could forgive her and carry on, as if nothing has happened.

Even though everything has happened.

DEAD STRAIGHT LINE

There are no easy choices.
My thoughts turn to Tanker.
What would he do?
He'd get his scales out and weigh the alternatives.
On one side – reasons to stay with Eden.
On the other side – reasons to leave Eden.
I'll get the scales out tonight.
Or maybe tomorrow.
Or maybe next week.
Take a deep breath and start running.
The path home is a winding one.
Life is never a dead straight line.

Author's Note and Acknowledgments
The story behind Rory

I've always been fascinated by risk. Why do people take them? And why do some of us fail to consider the consequences if things go wrong? That was the catalyst for *Dead Straight Line*. I wanted to explore what it means for a young guy like Rory to take a risk and to have to deal with the fall-out when an innocent game takes a terrible turn.

My stories are fiction, but in places, they're based on fact. The game Rory plays is the same one I played as a teenager. I'll never forget the queasy feeling in my stomach when my friend Andrew said we were going to head back to his house, in a dead straight line. Instead of taking paths we ran through back gardens and climbed over fences and hedges. It was exhilarating, scary and, looking back on it, quite stupid. Luckily, neither of us got hurt.

Another time I took a risk, things didn't play out so well. In my early twenties, I got into a car with some friends. We'd been drinking. I didn't put on my seatbelt. The car crashed and I went through the windscreen. I had cuts on my eyes and over a hundred stitches in my head. I was off work for three months. My forehead is still numb to this day. Thankfully, no-one was killed, but I still bear the scars from what happened on that sunny day in Newcastle all those years ago.

In a spilt second, things can go horribly wrong, which is what happens to Rory's reluctant game player, Eliot, paralysed after a fall while taking part in the game. Eliot's story was born from the experiences of my own family, helping our mum, who was confined to a wheelchair for the last few years of her life. For someone who'd been incredibly active, she found herself needing a wheelchair to get around. It came as both a shock and an eye-opener to our family, as the simplest things proved to be obstacles. But, like Eliot, she showed that positivity can shine through, even in the most difficult circumstances.

The story isn't only about risk, it's about trust, something that can be so hard to gain, and so easy to lose. As a result of playing Dead Straight Line, and injuring Eliot, Rory loses the trust of his family and friends. Both he and Eliot suffer in different ways and need to rebuild their lives.

I couldn't have written Rory's story without the help of others.

I'd like to thank the people at Combat Stress who gave me valuable insights into PTSD and the struggles of those suffering from the effects of military conflict. In particular, I'd like to thank Julian Barrett, a veteran of the Falklands, for his incredible stories about the war and particularly the battle for Mount Longdon.

A big thanks to David Eastham from the Spinal Injuries Association (SIA), for talking to me so openly about the accident that left him in a wheelchair at a young age, and how he has dealt with the obstacles and issues he's faced.

Then there are those who've helped me put this book into your hands – my fantastic agent Davinia Andrew-Lynch, the incredible editor and publisher Fiona Kennedy and the whole team at Zephyr – Abigail Kelly, Art Director Jessie Price, Naomi Greenwood, the fabulous publicist Laura Smythe, and last, but not least, Jon Gray for yet another eye-catching cover.

Malcolm Duffy
Surrey
August 2025

About the Author

Malcolm has been Creative Director at some of London's top advertising agencies, writing award-winning work for national and international brands.

It was while working as Creative Director of Comic Relief that he had the idea for his first novel, *Me Mam. Me Dad. Me.*, which was shortlisted for the Waterstones Children's Book Prize, as well as picking up a host of awards. This was followed by *Sofa Surfer*, nominated for the CILIP Carnegie medal, *Read Between the Lies*, selected by EmpathyLab as part of their Read for Empathy Collection, and *Seven Million Sunflowers*, a story about Ukrainian refugees living in Britain, which won The Federation of Children's Book Groups Award for Older Readers, as well as the Trinity Schools Book Award.

Born in Newcastle-upon-Tyne, Malcolm now lives in Surrey with his Kiwi wife Jann and daughters Tallulah and Tabi.

Discover more of Malcolm's books

WINNER of the Sheffield Children's YA Book Award 2019

WINNER of the Redbridge Children's Book Award 2019

Shortlisted for the Waterstone's Children's Book Award 2019

Sunday Times Children's Book of the Week

'A story with great heart, and wisdom, which shows the healing power of true friendship'
Ele Fountain, author of *Boy 87*

'Duffy has a talent for imparting serious ideas entertainingly'
Sunday Times, Children's Book of the Week

'Well-paced and highly engaging, readers will be surprised by more than one satisfying twist'
BookTrust, Book of the Month

'A grippingly unfolding domestic drama'
Sunday Times, Children's Book of the Week

WINNER of the FCBG Children's Book Award 2025, Older Readers' Category

'A memorable, moving, powerful book'
Irish Times

'This is an exercise in empathy that works hard to make readers empathetic too'
Sunday Times, Children's Book of the Week

Zephyr is an imprint of Bloomsbury Children's Books. At Zephyr we are proud to publish books you can read and re-read time and time again because they tell a brilliant story and because they entertain you.

X @_ZephyrBooks

◯ @_zephyrbooks

readzephyr.com

www.bloomsbury.com

ZEPHYR